"Surely you don't expect me to live with you!"

Georgie's voice faltered as she tried to continue. "I mean, it's not . . ."

"Not proper, Georgie?" Niklaas finished for her. "You forget, I was expecting a man, and since it's always been customary for the assistant to use my spare bedroom, no other arrangements were made."

"But . . . now you know—" she stammered.

"Georgie," he interrupted, "you've just spent most of our trip here trying to convince me you're not like other women. So presumably my presence won't be any threat to you, your reputation or your susceptibilities?" Niklaas's voice was softly quizzical as he took her chin in a gentle but firm grip. "That is so, isn't it? You are totally indifferent to men, aren't you, Georgie?"

"I am to you!" Georgie panicked, suddenly aware of the truth.

Annabel Murray has pursued many hobbies. She helped found an arts group in Liverpool, England, where she lives with her husband and two daughters. She loves drama: she appeared in many stage productions and went on to write an award-winning historical play. She uses all her experiences—holidays being no exception—to flesh out her characters' backgrounds and create believable settings for her romance novels.

Books by Annabel Murray

HARLEQUIN ROMANCE

2549—ROOTS OF HEAVEN
2558—KEEGAN'S KINGDOM
2596—THE CHRYSANTHEMUM AND THE SWORD
2612—VILLA OF VENGEANCE
2625—DEAR GREEN ISLE
2717—THE COTSWOLD LION
2782—THE PLUMED SERPENT
2819—WILD FOR TO HOLD
2843—RING OF CLADDAGH

HARLEQUIN PRESENTS

933—LAND OF THUNDER
972—FANTASY WOMAN
1029—NO STRINGS ATTACHED

Untamed Sanctuary

Annabel Murray

Harlequin Books

TORONTO • NEW YORK • LONDON
AMSTERDAM • PARIS • SYDNEY • HAMBURG
STOCKHOLM • ATHENS • TOKYO • MILAN

Original hardcover edition published in 1987
by Mills & Boon Limited

ISBN 0-373-17008-4

Harlequin Romance first edition February 1988

CHAPTER ONE

'IT's unlikely you'll be successful,' Paul Jonson warned his stepdaughter. 'It sounds to be very much the kind of job that will go to a man.'

'I don't see why!' Immediately Georgie's pointed chin set inflexibly, her small, slender figure too stiffening into obstinate rigidity. 'These days there shouldn't be any sexual discrimination and the advert said "person", not "man", and I *have* been short-listed.'

Wisely, Paul made no further comment, but confined himself in private to consoling his anxious wife.

'I'm not altogether sure they go in for sexual equality in some overseas countries, and even if they do, if they want a male vet for this job they'll appoint a man and be able to show good reason why. Anyway, it's almost certain the other applicants will have more experience to offer.'

'But suppose she *is* successful? It will mean her going away, right away! At least when she was at college . . .'

'Maggie, Maggie!' Paul said gently. 'Don't you see, this is a tremendous step forward? Two or three years ago, Georgie wouldn't even have dreamt of applying. But I've noticed a change in her lately. She's ready to stand on her own feet again, regained her self-confidence. You should be glad!'

'I am in one way, but it's been so nice this last year, her working with you, where we could keep an eye on her, just in case . . .'

'There isn't going to be any "just in case". Georgie may still have her fears deep down, indeed I'm sure she has. But she's learnt to cope with them by herself. This could be the final step in her complete cure.'

Maggie Jonson shook her head despairingly.

'You may be right; I hope you are. But I still wish Georgina had trained for a more *feminine* career, hairdressing or secretarial work. But she acts more like a boy than a girl. It's not right. At her age, she should be paying attention to her appearance, thinking of marriage.'

'Give her time, Maggie!' her husband advised.

'Time!' Maggie exploded. 'Time! You've been saying that ever since she was sixteen. She should have got over that . . . that business by now.'

'She will,' Paul comforted, 'when the right man comes along. It will take a very special man to win Georgie's trust.'

'And suppose he *never* comes along, this Mr Wonderful of yours?'

Paul shrugged. 'At least she'll have a satisfying career.'

The interviews were held in London, at the Ritz. Two other candidates had been short-listed, both male, one middle-aged, the other a few years older than Georgie.

As Paul Jonson had shrewdly guessed, Georgie had recently reached a decision. She was twenty-five, and it was now or never. Physically she was tremendously fit, and if her mind misgave her a little about the step she was taking, that was only natural. At least now she felt she could do it, whereas before ... She'd enjoyed working with her stepfather, had been grateful for the security of home. But Paul and Maggie were entitled to a life of their own, and the practice could not support two vets indefinitely.

She had given a lot of thought to her appearance. She knew her slight stature and fragile bone structure made her look younger than her years, so she had aimed for a mature, sensible look, her hair pulled up and backwards into a severe knot and an immaculately tailored trouser suit, calculated to proclaim her emancipation.

But these precautions were wasted on the young man sprawled negligently in the sitting-room of his hotel suite, a tall, thin pale young man, with bright marmalade hair and vivid green eyes. In his presence, Georgie felt immediately at ease. He presented no threat. Why, he was just like Roscoe, her favourite cat among the family's pets!

'Come in!' The bright, bold eyes saw straight through the camouflage she had adopted and instantly he was on his feet, holding out his hand, a hand she accorded a strong grip, but immediately released. 'I'm Dirk de Vries. Am I to understand you're applying for this position?' He sounded amused, incredulous, but certainly not displeased.

'Why not?' Georgie was immediately on the defensive, but it seemed there was no need.

'Why not indeed?' he murmured, his gaze frankly appreciative. 'I was expecting "Miss Jonson" to be a tough, middle-aged spinster, but—' his tone became thoughtful, '—if you're suitable ...' A strange glint lit the green eyes as he added, 'And I'd certainly like to see my chief vet's face! He can be an awkward swine where women are concerned,

but somehow I don't think you're likely to be
thrown by him.'

With a swift change of mood, Dirk de Vries
became businesslike, almost, Georgie thought, as if
he were suddenly eager to establish her credentials.

'You are a fully qualified vet, as you stated in your
application?'

'I am.' Coolly competent, Georgie presented
documentary evidence of her attention to chemis-
try, physics, biology and zoology, the mysteries of
physiology and parasitology. From these, she
explained, she had graduated to anatomy, surgery,
medicine, and a specialist course in exotic species.

'Very impressive,' he congratulated her. 'And
experience?'

'I've worked as my stepfather's assistant every
spare moment, and part of his practice incorporates
the local zoo.'

She answered further questions briskly but
comprehensively, gratified that at least he was
subjecting her to a rigorous interview, taking her
seriously, not dismissing her application out of
hand because of her sex, as her stepfather had
predicted, as she, secretly, had feared.

'And there's nothing to hold you back from
travelling? No fiancé or serious boy-friend?'

'Nothing like that.' Despite the endeavours of
many personable young men, Georgie remained
determinedly aloof, politely uninterested.

'Englishmen must be blind,' Dirk de Vries
commented. 'And now are there any questions
you'd like to ask me?'

'I can't help wondering,' she said frankly, 'why
you've come to England to make this appointment.
Surely you have vets in your country?'

'True,' he acknowleged. 'However, I was educated in England, and my chief vet did his training here. We both have a great admiration for your educational system. But it was he who urged me to employ an Englishman this time. Though in your case,' the strange expression crossed his face again, 'it seems it will be an Englishwoman.'

'Mr de Vries,' Georgie could not suppress her rising excitement, 'does this mean you're considering me for the job?'

'Yes. It's yours, subject to a month's trial on either side.' He stood up again, once more extending the narrow, almost fragile hand. 'Shall we shake on it? I shall look forward to furthering our acquaintance.' He attempted to retain her hand, an effort Georgie thwarted, his tone now expressing the admiration that, earlier, his eyes had revealed. 'And now, for a start, shall we celebrate your appointment? Will you lunch with me? I can tell you more about Marula and about the people you'll be working with.'

Despite her earlier show of confidence, her success still seemed slightly incredible to Georgie, when she related the outcome of her interview to Maggie and Paul Jonson.

'Congratulations,' Paul said sincerely, 'I'm very happy for you.'

'And he didn't mind in the least that I was a woman!' she announced triumphantly. She missed their significant exchange of glances.

'What's this Mr de Vries like?' asked her mother.

A reminiscent smile of amusement curved Georgie's lips as she recalled her first impression.

'Oh, he's a pussycat!'

Paul Jonson looked sharply at his stepdaughter.

'Cats have claws,' he said abruptly. 'I'm glad you feel up to taking this step Georgie. But don't, whatever you do, err on the side of over-confidence. Remember, he's a stranger and you'll be in a strange country for the first time . . . and that's another thing, you haven't told us where this job is going to take you.'

'I thought you'd never ask. That's the best part. I'm going to South Africa!'

'*South Africa!*' Dismayed, her mother echoed the words.

'Yes, to work in a game park, as assistant to their chief vet. Isn't it thrilling? I've always wanted to travel, only I've never dared before, and to work with exotic species.'

'A . . . a game park?' Mrs Jonson had paled. 'With . . . with wild animals?'

'Not the Kruger, surely?' Paul Jonson sounded impressed.

'No, of course not.' Georgie laughed at the idea. 'Apparently quite a few private landowners have established game parks of their own around the boundaries of the National Park. The de Vries family own one. They offer facilities for small safari and hunting parties. The work really needs two people, and they've just lost their assistant vet.'

'Lost?' quavered Mrs Jonson, with visions of man-eating lions.

'Moved on, Mum. In fact, he's gone to the Kruger. Probably,' Georgie added, 'because he didn't get on with the chief vet. According to Dirk de Vries he's a curmudgeonly old so-and-so, and he's a professed woman-hater.'

'And you think you can cope with that?' Paul

Jonson asked, knowing his stepdaughter's volatile temper, her touchy independence.

'For the sake of a job like this, I'll put up with anything and anyone,' she assured him. 'Besides, I'd rather work with a woman-hater than the other sort.'

'But when do you have to go?' Maggie Jonson asked.

'I fly to Johannesburg on the second of October.'

'Only two weeks? You'll be gone in *two weeks*!' her mother exclaimed. 'Oh, Paul!' She turned to her husband. 'Are you going to let her go off on this . . . this foolhardy . . .?'

'Let her? My dear, I don't see how I could stop her, even if I wanted to. She bears my name, I like to think she looks on me as her father, but even so, she's her own woman, not a child any more. In fact,' he said, a note of wistfulness entering his voice, 'I could almost envy her.'

Georgie's first hint of her destination was the thin, meandering line of light and dark water below, cutting through the bush—the River Limpopo, South Africa's northern boundary. Then there was the skyline of Johannesburg, tall, lean, silvery skyscrapers, soaring like spaceships, housing the banks, mining houses and other giant business concerns.

She was swiftly through Immigration, very much aware that now she was in another country. Announcements over the loudspeaker were in two languages, as were the signs. '*Slegs vir Blanks*', one read, 'Europeans only'.

The Carlton Centre, fifty-two storeys high, a great office, shopping and amusement complex, also boasted a huge hotel where Georgie was to spend her first night and where Dirk de Vries had arranged to collect her the next day. Judging him by his choice of hotels, here and in England, Georgie gathered that her employer was a very wealthy man indeed.

After a meal she sauntered round the complex, its piazzas and pools, ice-rink and exhibition centre, and retired to bed in a state of pleasant exhaustion, tinged with anticipation. Yesterday she had left an increasingly chilly, autumnal England. But here it was spring, and tomorrow her new life would really begin, new horizons open up, the shadowed past left far behind.

At ten o'clock next morning, overnight bag in hand, Georgie descended to the hotel foyer. She had dressed for travelling in workmanlike jeans and a checked shirt which echoed the deep blue of her eyes. To her disappointment there was no sign of her employer. Only one man stood in the reception area, his back towards the lift from which she'd emerged. A tall man, over six feet, dressed in khaki bush shirt and shorts, he swung round as the lift doors purred to a gentle close. As he turned, involuntarily Georgie's eyes widened. She was not as a rule given to superlatives, but—purely academically speaking, of course—his was one of the most arresting faces she had ever seen.

It wasn't that he was classically handsome, for his bronzed face was angular, lean to the point of asceticism. On either side of an uncompromisingly straight nose, vivid green eyes met her startled gaze. He gave her a brief, polite smile, even white teeth in sharp contrast to his tan, then turned away to continue the restless pacing in which he had been engaged.

Georgie sat down on one of the comfortable elegant settees and prepared for a wait. In his pacing the tall man's gaze encountered hers once or twice, and finally he moved towards her, his long stride easily paced. She took a deep, steadying breath as he sat down beside her.

'Irritating business, isn't it, waiting around for people? My contact's late too.' His deep voice held all the fascination of the South African accent, a cadence quite unlike any other. 'You are waiting for someone, I presume?'

She nodded speechlessly. Though deliberately reserved with men, she wasn't normally shy, but this stranger was a little over-awing, something quite outside her experience. Her lowered eyes registered strong, muscular legs and arms, deeply tanned and lightly coated with soft, reddish down, shades lighter than his thick auburn hair. Hastily she looked away, transferring her gaze back to his face.

'Your first time in South Africa?' Niklaas van der Walt noted with detached pleasure what he saw as her gentle, almost demure manner. This girl would not take his polite passing-of-the-time amiss. He studied her far from perfect features, which tended towards the sharp rather than the rounded norm of femininity. But looks, as he had good reason to know, weren't everything, and on the bonus side her skin, innocent of make-up, was fresh and wholesome-looking, her mouth wide with a hint of vulnerability. He found himself hoping, for her sake, that her contact would turn up soon.

'Yes,' she was answering his question, 'I've

always wanted to visit South Africa, but I never dreamt I'd have the chance of actually working here.' Despite her reserve, she couldn't prevent her eyes from sparkling with enthusiasm.

Such eyes, he thought, with an almost tender amusement. They were her greatest asset, almost eating up her delicate features. The idea of this slight child working for a living, in this climate! What as, he wondered idly—children's nanny, maybe? That was one of the most common reasons for English girls working abroad.

'You'll be working here, in Jo'burg, I suppose?' He found himself still held by the large, deep blue eyes, fringed with sooty lashes, that contrasted strongly with the silvery fairness of her hair, worn in a bouncy ponytail.

'Oh no!' There was a proud little lift to her head as she spoke. 'I want to see the *real* South Africa. I'm going to a place called Marula. Do you know of it?'

'As it happens,' he said slowly, 'I do. But what exactly . . .?'

'Oh good, then you'll know Dirk de Vries!' The excited words bubbled over, interrupting him. 'I'm going to work for him.'

'What as?' The words were splintered ice, and though there was no reason why his change of mood from comradely to hostile should bother her, Georgie found that it did.

'As . . . as a vet,' she said, not knowing that her puzzled regret showed in face and eyes.

'Would you mind telling me your name?' The deep voice was still cold and stern, and she felt that he waited tensely for her answer, which now she hesitated to give him.

'G . . . Georgie. Georgie Jonson. I . . .' Her voice trailed away as his eyes narrowed to green slits.

'Good God! It can't be! But it's too incredible to be a coincidence. Dirk hired *you*?' There was a note in his voice difficult to interpret. He sounded annoyed, disapproving. But there was a more subtle inflexion . . . disappointment? He didn't wait for her answer, his tone becoming brusquer. 'Miss Jonson, would you like some advice?'

'If it's relevant.' The swift alteration in him had put Georgie on her guard.

'Oh, it's relevant all right. South Africa's no place for you. *Marula's* no place for you. You wouldn't last a day. Go home, Miss Jonson. Find yourself a job, if in fact you are a vet, in some practice where the clients are pampered pussies and overfed lapdogs. We deal in larger game at Marula.

'I know that!' Georgie elevated her chin at him. 'And I *am* a vet. Why should you think I'm not? I've also studied the treatment of larger mammals and exotic species.'

'Even so, you'll hardly have encountered lions or elephants.' And as she would have interrupted him with a denial, 'I repeat, go home.' It was said matter-of-factly, without apparent malice, but it was an unpardonable presumption on the part of a stranger.

'May I ask,' Georgie's temper was aroused now, the demure girl Niklaas had imagined her to be no longer in evidence, 'what all this has to do with *you*? You pick me up, pry into my affairs, and then proceed to tell me what I should or shouldn't do!'

Niklaas stood up. He felt edgy, uncharacteristically irritable. He hadn't relished this trip to Jo'burg anyway. He rarely left Marula if he could help it.

There was plenty of space there, space to get away from people. There was tranquillity, and there were the animals to which he had dedicated his life. Animals were uncomplicated, unambiguous. True, they had the power to wound, but only physically, not emotionally. What the hell was Dirk up to this time, and with this innocent-looking child, for she couldn't be much more? Or was she as innocent as she seemed? And why the hell should he feel any concern, get involved? He tried not to let his irritation show in his voice, tried to convince her.

'Believe me, my advice is well-meant. You're a mere child . . .'

'I am *not* a child!' Georgie sparked back at him. 'I'm twenty-five and . . .'

'Good lord,' he said softly, 'and I'd have placed you around eighteen, twenty at the most. Look, Miss Jonson, you must accept that I know what I'm talking about. I know Marula and I know Dirk de Vries, probably far better than you do. The park is no place for a woman, a fact that's been proved more than once, and as for de Vries . . .'

'Stop it!' Now it was Georgie who jumped up, her lips trembling, but with anger. 'I don't know who you are, or what right you think you have to talk like this, but I won't hear a word against Dirk. He was kind enough to offer me a job I wanted very much. We signed a contract, a month's trial on either side, and I intend to abide by it.' By this time the whole of her slender form was shaking with outrage.

'Miss Jonson, please,' Niklaas extended a large, bronzed hand, placed it placatingly on her bare arm, 'I think it's time I introduced myself.'

'I don't *want* to know your name!' She flinched away from him, further annoyed by the familiar gesture, the brief brush of flesh on flesh, offending her trigger-sensitive nerves. Despite her mistrust of all men except her stepfather, she had recognised at first glance this man's potential attraction, his magnetism, had been glad their paths would cross only briefly. Then, during their conversation, she had found herself appreciating his straightforward, impersonal manner. Despite her accusation that he had 'picked her up', there had been no attempt on his part at over-familiarity. But just that momentary touch of his fingers had confirmed his masculine appeal, a virility that made her shrink from him.

'I'm Niklaas van der Walt,' he persisted, 'de Vries's chief vet. He owns Marula, but the animals are under my care. I'm here, as I thought, to meet a Mr George Jonson.' He watched with interest as the colour of realisation flooded her face, watched the deep blue eyes widen in dismay.

This was the man against whom Dirk had warned her, with whom she must work?

'You'll find him a cold, unapproachable man,' Dirk had said, 'totally, irrationally prejudiced, of course, where women are concerned. The only living creatures he seems to care for are the animals.'

But she hadn't found this man cold to begin with, not, in fact, until she'd revealed her name, her destination, and besides, she'd expected the man Dirk had pictured for her to be elderly, desiccated, not young and disconcertingly virile. The glance from eyes like angry sapphires was meant to wither him where he stood.

'Dirk told me you'd be against his employing a woman. But he also said there was far too much work for one vet. If you're really dedicated, you'll put the animals' welfare before your own chauvinistic prejudices. I suppose you're one of these insufferably arrogant men who won't admit that a woman can be as good at her work as a man.'

'Not at all,' he replied deflatingly, his deliberate calm only increasing her own resentment, almost to flashpoint. 'But as you rightly suggest, I *do* have to put the animals first. A female assistant could be a liability. Many of the animals I have to treat are dangerous, and,' he added obscurely, 'there are other, less obvious hazards at Marula. I haven't time to act as wet-nurse-cum-bodyguard.'

Georgie drew herself up, wishing in vain for additional inches to give her retort more dignity. How could this man recognise the indestructible resilience of her body, the deliberately cultivated, indomitable will that drove it? No one, unless they had actually witnessed it, ever believed that she had handled large, intractable horses, had found the physical strength to turn and deliver breech-presentation calves.

'If I work with you——' she began, then stopped and corrected herself, her generous mouth set into obstinate lines. Whatever Niklaas van der Walt's objections, the job *was* hers. 'When I work with you, my safety will be my own responsibility. I'm pretty handy with a rifle, and I'm not given to panicking or clinging to the nearest man for protection. I like to be independent.'

And he'd like to be able to believe her, Niklaas thought, his eyes appraising her slim, boyish grace. There was an ineffably touching gallantry about her defiance of him. She appeared undaunted by what must seem to her to be an unwarrantedly hostile reception in a strange country. But he'd learnt long ago to suspect the motives of his employer and those of anyone connected with him. And even if this girl were as well qualified as she claimed to be, her connections with de Vries above reproach, Niklaas still didn't relish the idea of her working at Marula. He'd been perfectly sincere when he'd told her it was no place for a woman. His features contorted bitterly as he recalled the convincing evidence he'd received of that.

Georgie took his expression for disbelief of her claim, of a continuing distaste for her appointment, but she stood her ground, waiting for his inevitable attempt at further discouragement. She wasn't afraid of anything he might have to say, she told herself, nor could he force her to leave South Africa. However, he seemed to have realised the ineffectiveness of his objections, for, with a swift glance at his watch, he appeared to capitulate.

'OK, so you're staying for the moment, but only because I can't waste any more time trying to make you see sense. But if I'm dissatisfied with your work, friend of Dirk's or not, you'll hear about it, and so will he.'

'I'm not a friend of his!'

'Let's get a move on.' Ignoring her denial, he held out a hand for her suitcase, but with an impatient gesture Georgie rejected his assistance. She'd made a declaration of independence, and the proof of that claim could start right here and now. She would show this cold, arrogant man just what she was made of!

A mudstained, tarpaulin-covered jeep looked incongruous parked amidst expensive limousines. Now, impatiently overcoming her resistance, Niklaas seized her luggage and flung it into the back of the vehicle. He was left-handed, she noticed.

She took her place in the passenger seat of the narrow cab and the jeep started away with a jerk, giving some indication of the still exacerbated state of the driver's feelings, then pulled out into the road in a wide sweep, heading out of town.

Georgie stole a surreptitious glance at him. He was intent upon his driving and, she suspected, his reflections, which did not appear to please him. In profile, his features were firm and decisive, yet, surprisingly, seen from this angle there was also a fine sensitivity of countenance. He was not just a man of action, she guessed, but—and she recognised a tendency similar to her own—one who communed deeply with himself, too deeply, perhaps.

'Why did you meet me instead of Dirk?' she ventured. After all, they had to work together. Their relationship might as well be a civil one.

'I'm sorry to disappoint you.' He didn't sound in the least regretful, only ironic. 'But he's away, down at the Cape.' He angled her a sharp glance. 'I notice you're very free with his first name. Just how long have you known de Vries?'

'I met him for the first time at the interview,' she said, stiffening indignantly. He was implying again that she hadn't gained the job purely on merit. 'He asked me to call him Dirk.'

'And "Georgie" is short for Georgina, I suppose?' Georgie had always preferred the shortened version of her name, but there was something in the way the deep, accented voice pronounced 'Georgina' that gave the name a graciousness, a richer meaning. 'That's where the error arose, of course,

Dirk's damned spidery hand.' He lapsed into silence once more, but Georgie didn't care, she told herself. There was plenty to occupy her in her new surroundings.

It was the jacaranda season, and the magnificent residential suburbs of the ridges surrounding Johannesburg were laced with avenues of blue-mauve blossoms. Parks and gardens blazed with exotic splashes of colour, making the contrast as they reached the open veld all the more striking.

Here the landscape was beyond even her imaginings, tremendous, sparsely vegetated. An immense, incredibly blue sky, broken by theatrical clouds, encompassed this strange new world. As they travelled on through the afternoon they passed the occasional isolated farm, or dusty *dorp*—village—drowsing in the sun, but saw very little sign of life, particularly wild life.

'Where are all the animals?' asked Georgie. She had arrived in South Africa with highly charged ideas concerning its primitiveness, and her disillusion sounded in her voice.

'There are very few wild animals—wild, that is, in the sense of roaming the countryside at will.' At least he'd answered her, a little of the coldness gone from his voice. 'A hundred years ago, yes, they teemed in their millions, right on the very place where Jo'burg stands. Nowadays they're only to be seen in game sanctuaries and National Parks.'

He darted a brief, shrewd glance at her absorbed profile. She was taking an enjoyment in her surroundings which could not possibly be feigned. Maybe he should give her the benefit of the doubt? Often enough well-meaning friends had tried to tell him that not all women were like Lysette, but he had always preferred not to put their theories to the test.

'How long will it take us to get to Marula?' Georgie's cool, pleasant, English voice interrupted his thoughts.

'Three days.'

'*Three days!* Of *this*?' Her gesture encompassed the barren terrain, the close confines of the jeep, which was certainly not built for comfort.

'If you really want to work in South Africa, you'll need to get used to its disadvantages.' Infuriatingly, Niklaas van der Walt sounded amused by her dismay. 'One of which is the long distances between one place and another. We shan't have to camp in the open,' he added, 'if that's what worrying you?'

'I wasn't worrying,' she began, indignant that he should think her such a feeble creature, but he went on, ignoring her protest.

'Tonight we stop off at a native village, where they know me, and push on tomorrow to the Kruger. All being well, we'll be in Marula late the following day.'

'Why aren't we going straight there?' Georgie was anxious to have Dirk de Vries confirm, for the benefit of the man at her side, that there had been no question of undue influence or nepotism in her appointment. She was keen, too, to begin the work to which she looked forward.

'Because I promised to look in on a former colleague and I can't spare the time to drop you off first.'

Three days' journey, with only the company of a man who, for his own obscure reasons, disapproved of her. It was a prospect that caused her nerves to vibrate with alarm, but it was something she must endure with outward philosophy at least, if she were not to deepen his prejudice against her.

A dusk of violet and dove-grey was enfolding the veld as they approached the native village, but the moon bathed the land in radiance, making thorn trees cast long, exotic shadows. A thick thorn fence, a deterrent to predatory wild life, surrounded the village, and once within its perimeter Georgie was relieved to step down from the passenger seat, flexing her legs, cramped with the long drive.

Was this really Georgie Jonson, hundreds of miles away from everything and everyone familiar to her, Georgie Jonson, living and breathing Africa? she wondered incredulously half an hour later, as she and Niklaas sat cross-legged round the villagers' fire, sharing their meal of *skaapribbetjies*, sheep's ribs, and *mielipap*, a thick maize porridge. Yes. It was incredible, but it was true. But her euphoria was short-lived, when she found the experience was to include sharing one of the small *tamboekie*— grass-thatched mud huts—with her companion. Her outraged refusal fell upon unsympathetic ears. Moreover, Niklaas treated her protests with amusement.

'That's typical of women,' he said mockingly. 'They go on *ad nauseam* about equality, but when they receive equal treatment they're the first to complain. Good God, girl, it's unusual for there to be one hut available, let alone two. You might very well have had to sleep in the open. I often do.'

'In that case,' she retorted, stung by his male arrogance, 'if you're so used to it, why don't you sleep outside tonight?' At the thought of sharing such confined quarters with a man, the old fear fluttered in her heart.

His speculative green eyes, his lopsided grin, only served to inflame her annoyance, to which she hoped he would attribute her visible tremors.

'If all this reluctance for my company stems from maidenly modesty, perhaps I can reassure you. Don't forget, I didn't contrive this situation. I was expecting you to be a man, and you flatly denied wanting any preferential treatment.'

'It's not my fault you made a stupid mistake about my name. But you're right, I don't expect any concessions. In fact, I can't think why it didn't occur to me before, if you can sleep outside, so can I.' Then she added, with a touch of deliberate malice, 'After all, if you can put up with the hardship at your age, I certainly can.' She had no real idea of his age, but put him at a good ten years older than herself. She had hoped to needle him, but he remained infuriatingly calm, unimpressed by either her show of independence or her taunt. In fact, she had a feeling he was enjoying watching her talk herself into a situation from which there was no easy retreat.

Certainly he made no attempt to dissuade her, but simply dragged two sleeping-bags and two blankets from the back of the jeep and casually tossed one of each towards her.

'Enjoy your first night under the African stars. By the time you reach my "advanced years"'—he sounded lightly amused—could nothing pique the dratted man? 'perhaps you'll have learnt to accept the gifts the gods provide. They occur rarely enough. Goodnight.'

The heat of the day, the warm evening, terminating in the curiously cosy atmosphere round the fire, had not prepared Georgie for the penetrating chill of the African night. Nor had she been prepared for the feeling of utter loneliness, as the inhabitants of the village retired. Without human company, the sounds of the night seemed to grow louder and more ominous, as did her realisation of having made a stupid mistake, and all because Niklaas van der Walt had succeeded in getting under her skin, whereas he himself seemed to have a hide like a rhinoceros.

Why did he have this effortless knack of provoking her? She'd been prepared to deal firmly and tactfully with a grumpy, middle-aged man with a dislike of female company, so what was different? The difference was, she had no idea how to treat a man like Niklaas. He was something quite outside her experience. She couldn't bring herself to placate him. It smacked of female subservience to the male. Besides, she had the feeling it would make no impression on him, other than to confirm his obvious belief in the inferiority of women. From now on, she resolved, she would curb her impetuous tongue. Cool indifference, which had served her successfully enough in the past, would be her watchword.

Frogs and crickets filled the air with croaking and chirping. Somewhere a bird called with an eerie screech. Grunts and weird animal sounds carried over great distances on the night air. Was the thorn enclosure really capable of keeping out predators? That barely perceptible rustling sound, was it a wild beast, even now creeping up on her, the silence the electric one before the final, fatal leap?

A movement close by that was not an imagined one made Georgie jerk upright, emitting a shrill cry

as she did so that set the camp dogs barking. The
next moment she was swept up, complete with
sleeping-bag and blanket, and she registered the
fact that at least her assailant was human, not
animal. But who? She struggled, fighting with fists
and feet.

'Shut up and keep still,' a deep, accented voice
adjured her.

'Niklaas!' Relief warred with resentment at the
fright he'd given her, and she didn't realise she'd
used his first name.

'I thought I'd better check up on you,' he
muttered gruffly as he dumped her in a corner of the
hut, 'and it's as well I did. You're numb with cold
and as nervous as a kitten!' He was on his knees
beside her, chafing the cold hands that had beaten
so frantically against his chest.

'I . . . I . . .' Georgie tried to deny her fear, her
frozen body, but her teeth chattered inarticulately.
She couldn't even get the words out to tell him to
leave her alone.

After a few minutes Niklaas ceased his ministrations, and dragged his own sleeping-bag over beside
hers. Sliding into it, he edged closer, until his body
trapped hers against the wall of the hut.

'Relax!' he commanded, as involuntarily she
tried to jerk away. 'Get some sleep.'

'I . . . I can't,' she stuttered. 'I . . . I can't sleep
with you . . . here, like this. Please g-go away.'

He raised himself on one elbow.

'You're really scared of me, aren't you?' he said
incredulously. 'For God's sake, whatever reason
have I given you? Listen to me and listen good. I've
had a long day, I'm tired and I've absolutely no
inclinations in the direction you seem to fear. In

fact, you're not even my type. Now goodnight!'

For a while Georgie was tensely still, but then she remembered Dirk's statement that Niklaas was impervious to women, and the sound of his deep, regular breathing seemed to give testimony of that lack of interest. To herself she could admit that she was glad of the warmth emanating from him, from the strong arm that encircled and immobilised her.

But what an enigma this man was. Since his albeit unwilling acceptance of Dirk's *fait accompli*, he had shown her nothing but cool, amused courtesy, and she could do no other than believe him as proof against the fact of her femininity as he was against her taunts. He annoyed her, he confused her, yet she felt that beneath his impenetrable exterior, basically he was a kind man, or he wouldn't have concerned himself with her comfort.

Cradled in human warmth, the thick walls of the hut deadening the night cries of the veld, Georgie slept.

CHAPTER TWO

'WELL, at least you have one advantage over a male room-mate. You don't snore.' Niklaas leant on one elbow, looking down into the wide, surprised eyes. He guessed that, for a moment, Georgie had wondered where she was, and he saw memory return in a hot rush of embarrassment, increasing the colour in her already sleep-flushed cheeks, saw alarm flare as she tried to edge away from him and found it impossible.

Seen like this, he thought critically, she wasn't bad-looking, and her nearness in the night, the consciousness of her femininity, an awareness of which attribute he'd thought long since beaten down, deliberately sublimated in his work, had not been unpleasant, if a little disturbing. He wondered idly what her reaction would be if he were to bend his head and kiss the soft lips that had not yet returned to their daytime determination.

Realising by the reactions of his own body just where these unwanted thoughts were leading, he jerked away, informing Georgie crisply that if they were to reach their next objective, she had best bestir herself.

Georgie had not been unaware of the tension implicit in those few moments of silence. The intent expression in his eyes had telegraphed some inscrutable message, and for a frozen, horrified instant she had actually thought he was going to kiss her. Ridiculous, she told herself. Why should he want to do that? She had obviously misinterpreted the whole incident.

'Know anything about the National Park?' Niklaas asked, as they drove away from their overnight accommodation.

'A bit. It was Paul Kruger's idea, wasn't it, the Boer President?'

'Mmm. Thank goodness he did have the foresight, or there'd be even less wild life than there is.'

'And you'd be out of a job!'

'More importantly, life would be that much less rich.' He returned a repressive reply to her light remark. And she'd begun to think he had a sense of humour!

'Have you ever worked at the Kruger?' She steered the conversation back on to safe ground.

'No, apart from my years of training I've always worked and lived at Marula. The Kruger's quite a different kettle of fish, much larger. If you can visualise it, it's about the size of Wales, with literally thousands of tourists through it during the season, and only a portion of it is open at any one time. Certain sections are completely inaccessible to the public, so that the natural ecology isn't disturbed.'

'And you've never had any ambition to move on to a larger undertaking?'

'Marula is my home,' he said simply, 'my life. But I wouldn't expect you to understand that.'

'Why not?' Georgie retorted. 'I understand perfectly. My stepfather is a vet and he feels exactly the same way about his practice, even though it's on a humbler scale than yours.'

'That's the nature of a dedicated man.'

'Women can be dedicated too!' Georgie said hotly.

'Can they?' He didn't sound convinced. 'What made you want to work in South Africa, Georgie?' And before she had time to reply he added, with a suspicious quirk to the corner of his mouth, 'After last night, it does seem unnecessarily formal to call you Miss Jonson.'

'Oh!' Georgie coloured up and was ready with an outraged retort to the effect that he needn't get any ideas, when he completely disarmed her by letting that quirk develop into a wide engaging smile, which so transformed his usually stern face that she found herself instead answering his question earnestly.

'I've always wanted to travel and to work with animals.' She gave a reminiscent smile. 'I'm afraid my stepfather had to put up with a lot from me when I was small. I was always bringing home small, wild creatures that had been injured. Sometimes he was able to cure them, sometimes not.'

'And like all small girls, when they died you wept buckets?' he hazarded.

'So?' Georgie was immediately defensive. 'I was only a child then, and if you think I'm likely to behave emotionally now, you're wrong?'

'Your parents encouraged you to become a vet?' Niklaas sounded genuinely interested, she thought cautiously. With this man she was becoming increasingly wary of verbal traps.

'Not my mother,' she admitted, 'she thought it wasn't very ladylike, but my stepfather helped me all he could, especially after ...' She stopped abruptly.

'After what?'

'Oh—er—nothing really. He just thought an absorbing career would be good for me.'

'Whereabouts in England do you come from?'

'Yorkshire.'

'I know it,' he surprised her by saying. 'I've been to York Minster and I've tramped the Yorkshire moors. You'll find Africa very different, the landscape, the climate. It's hard for European women to adjust.'

'I'll cope,' Georgie said with cheerful obstinacy, and Niklaas found himself almost believing that she would. Almost.

They were to stay overnight at the Kruger National Park, in one of the rest camps normally provided for the tourists.

'And,' Niklaas said drily, 'since it's nearly the end of the season, you can have the choice of twenty or so *rondavels* to yourself.'

'I wouldn't have shared with you last night,' she retorted immediately, 'if you hadn't made me.'

'No,' he agreed, 'that's a nasty little streak of pride you have.' She glared at him, but his smile was meant to take the sting out of the words. 'If I hadn't come out to you, you'd probably have been found this morning dead of cold, or fright.'

The colleague Niklaas had arranged to call on was Hendrik Beit, an open-faced, bespectacled young man of about Georgie's own age, delighted to see his visitors. He made Georgie especially welcome.

'Are you a vet too?' she asked.

'Yes. I was Niklaas's assistant for a while. But I'm more interested in the scientific aspect, animal behaviourism and ecology.' He turned to Niklaas. 'It was good of you to take the trouble to call in with the statistics I wanted on Marula.'

The walls of his office were covered with maps—
density of game, variety, migration patterns, all
recorded in detail, as were incidence of disease,
drought areas, fire-breaks, feeding grounds, water-
holes and innumerable other factors relevant to the
study and protection of the reserve's population.

Seeing Georgie's genuine fascination, Hendrik
began upon an animated explanation of his work,
from which he was only recalled by Niklaas's
restless movement and impatient exclamation.

'We do have our own scientists at Marula, you
know!'

'Sorry van der Walt.' The dark-haired young man
flushed. 'But it's not often I get a chance to show off
to an attractive woman, and an intelligent one at
that.'

To Georgie's discomfort, the young Afrikaaner
continued to pay her a considerable amount of
attention during the remainder of their stay, which,
to no avail, he pressed Niklaas to extend. He
invited her to visit him again, and declared his
intention of calling in at Marula at the very first
opportunity.

'That's one young idiot,' growled Niklaas, as they
left early next morning, 'who hasn't yet discovered
that a woman out here means trouble for a man.'

'Not *this* woman,' Georgie asserted with certain
knowledge, though she had no hope of his believing
her. Despite his apparent mellowing, Niklaas, she
realised, was just as opposed to her presence, still
unconvinced of her capabilities, of her ability to fit
into her new environment. Obviously argument,
even reasoned argument, was wasted breath.
Actions spoke louder than words, and Georgie

resolved that before her acquaintance with Niklaas van der Walt was very much older he would have cause to eat his words.

It was growing late, the hour before dusk, when they approached the entrance to the de Vries Park, and the sunset colours were quite spectacular. Used to England's smaller safari parks, Georgie hadn't expected just this single pole across the road, with only two Africans in casual attendance.

'Surely the animals must stray,' she puzzled, 'so how does it work?'

'Flexibly. Elephants and some of the larger carnivores have learnt to know the limits of their own park, much as the domestic tomcat knows his territory. They know they're safe there from human interference. If any of the big cats do stray over the border for a night's hunting, they take good care to be back inside the park again before dawn.' His flow of words stopped abruptly. 'But you're probably not interested in all that.'

'Of course I am.' Why should he doubt it?

'I suppose Dirk wrote to you, told you what arrangements he'd made for your accommodation?' Georgie shook her head and Niklaas swore feelingly. 'Feckless, irresponsible . . .' For a moment she thought he was referring to her, and her hackles rose. 'That's just like de Vries, does something on impulse, then leaves everyone else to sort out the mayhem he's created.'

'So what will I do?'

'I suppose I'll have to sort something out, temporarily.' He didn't sound very pleased at the prospect, and a weary Georgie found her normal optimism flagging a little. It wasn't going to be as easy as her sanguine hopes had led her to expect, to work with Marula's senior vet, overcome his prejudice.

Beyond the barrier there were warning signs, written in two languages, warning visitors to stay in their cars, that elephants were dangerous. Tourists, Niklaas explained, had to be inside their fenced-in camps before dark, and remain shut in all night until the gates reopened at first light.

As she had been on the veld, Georgie was struck by the immense quiet. Here, at least, she had expected to see the beasts she'd travelled so many miles to work with. Then suddenly, just as she'd given up hope, she saw him. Only feet from the track, silhouetted against the pink light, white lines on his silver-grey body, his head crowned with fine, spiralling, lyre-shaped horns ... a bull kudu, nibbling the leaves of a low-growing group of trees. Georgie gave a little gasp of awe.

'Oh, look, Niklaas—look!' To her, this very first sight of a wild animal in its natural surroundings was a revelation. It was so different from seeing an animal in a zoo, a quiet, apathetic prisoner. Here, in his own territory, the bull was alert yet self-confident, a superb spectacle. Georgie's enthusiasm bubbled over and she sought to share it with Niklaas.

'Zoos!' he said tersely. 'I hate the places. Animals should live as nature intended, wild and free. And,' he added obscurely, 'it's not such a bad idea for men either.'

'What about women?' Georgie challenged.

'Women?' His voice was reflective, then he shook his head. 'No, in the end women only want one thing, the security of marriage, the bright lights of civilisation and the man who can afford to provide them.'

'Not me!' Georgie averred. Since the age of sixteen she'd known that marriage was not for her.

'Not you?' enquired Niklaas ironically, disbelievingly.

Georgie shook her head emphatically. She shivered, and then, as she had been able to do—not immediately, but for at least the last five years—she thrust the subject from her.

'Are we anywhere near Dirk's house yet?' she asked. 'He said his home was just within the park limits.'

'We're well beyond his place now.'

'But shouldn't I be reporting to him, or . . .?'

'I told you, the de Vrieses are away. What's your interest there anyway?' A sideways glance, and that chilly, hostile note was back in Niklaas's voice, a note she'd hoped had vanished for ever.

'None,' she asserted, 'except that he's my employer.' Also, she thought, the problem of her accommodation had not been solved. Surely that was Dirk's province? 'But where will I be staying?'

'Certainly not at the de Vries place.' Again that swift look, and Georgie's face warmed with annoyance.

'I didn't expect for one moment that I would be!'

'No? But it must have occurred to you that de Vries is a very rich man and that female company is rather limited out here?'

'Just what are you implying?' she enquired tautly.

'I never imply, Georgie.' His voice sounded oddly weary. 'I've always found it best to come straight to the point. I can't believe, for instance, that you were the only suitable candidate for this job, and I can't help asking myself just why de Vries chose you. And I feel I ought to warn you, just because he did, not to get the wrong idea.' Despite his claim to bluntness, Niklaas hesitated before concluding. 'He's not likely to marry you, no matter how friendly you are.'

Georgie gasped. How dared he make such completely unwarranted assumptions?

'I told you,' she said acidly, 'I'm not interested in marriage, to Dirk or to anyone else. I didn't spend all those years studying, qualifying, just to give it up to be at some man's beck and call.'

'I seem to have heard those words before somewhere,' Niklaas said wryly, 'and seen them disproved.'

'You,' Georgie croaked, 'are insufferable! You've absolutely no reason to doubt what I say. You know nothing about me, and whatever you may think I have not come here to "set my cap" at Dirk!'

'I hope you mean that,' gravely. 'This is a remote sort of life. Dirk, of course, can afford to get away from it whenever the urge takes him, employees can't. It happens to suit me that way. But for a woman it's hard, Georgie. It can be a dangerous life, and above all it's real, no romantic idyll, and I've yet to meet the woman who could stick it out.'

She ground her teeth, biting back a stronger retort. Cool indifference, Georgie, she reminded herself.

'Then you're in for a surprise, Mr van der Walt, because you've just met her.'

The jeep braked before a large gate set in a thorn hedge and, having negotiated it, drew up in front of a long, low building, its outline blurred by the dusk. But for a moment Georgie ignored her surroundings. Niklaas had flicked on the cab light, and she was too busy staring defiantly into the hard, bronzed face turned towards her.

'You may or may not be capable of endurance, but I'm not easily convinced these days by a woman. Tell me, Georgie,' his manner became earnest, 'what are you going to do for a social life? Women like dressing up. There are no occasions here for that, unless you're in with the de Vrieses. What will you do when the loneliness gets to you? What will you do with your spare time?'

Georgie's eyes did not drop before the probing green gaze, nor did she allow the irritation she felt to reveal itself in her voice. She had realised that any show of annoyance was a victory for him.

'I like a challenge, mental or physical. As to a social life, I shan't miss that, since my studies didn't leave me all that much opportunity for one. As to spare time,' she added scornfully, 'anyone who can't find some activity or interest to fill their leisure hours has to be a pretty shallow person.'

'You may be interested,' Niklaas drawled drily, 'to know that my wife found herself so totally incapable of filling her hours that she left!'

'Oh!' Georgie flushed. 'I'm sorry, I didn't mean—I didn't know you were . . .'

'Really?' sarcastically. 'You mean that among the intimate details de Vries gave you of my character, he omitted to tell you that little gem, that I wasn't capable of sustaining my wife's affection and loyalty?'

Georgie felt mortified by her own tactlessness. Even though Dirk hadn't said anything, she should have guessed, she supposed that a man of Niklaas's age and attractiveness would not have remained single. She could certainly imagine him being a difficult man to live with. So now he was divorced, she presumed. She didn't like to ask.

'Wh-where are we?' she stammered instead. 'What's this place?'

'My bungalow.'

'*Your* bungalow? But . . .'

'It's always been the custom for the assistant to use my spare bedroom, and since I was expecting a man, and Dirk didn't see fit to make arrangements before he rushed off to the delights of civilisation . . .'

'But surely, now you know . . . I mean . . . it's not . . .' Her voice faltered away as, too late, she anticipated his reaction.

'Not proper, because you're a woman? But, Georgie, you've just spent most of the past three days trying to convince me that you're not like other women. So presumably my presence won't be any threat to you, your reputation or your susceptibilities?' Niklaas's voice was softly quizzical, and all at once Georgie had the panic-stricken sensation that the cab had shrunk to half its original dimensions.

'That is so, isn't it?' he said. 'I'm not mistaken?' A large hand took her chin in a gentle but firm grip and she sat paralysed, unable to move. 'You are totally indifferent to men, aren't you, Georgie?'

If she agreed to such a sweeping generalisation, or, even stronger, told him the truth, that she detested men, he wouldn't believe her. There was a surer, safer way of deflecting his interest from the subject.

'No, but I am to you.' Her panic was increasing, so that she found it hard to conceal. There was something in the touch of his hand, warm and hard against her face, that set off a primitive warning system, sending ripples of alarm along her central nervous system. And he *knew*. He knew just what he was doing to her, she was sure of it. It was as if he were conducting a coldly analytical experiment.

But as suddenly as he had taken hold of her, she was free and he was sliding out of the jeep.

'You'd better come and see where you'll be living, at least temporarily.'

He sounded so certain that the stipulated trial period would result in her departure. As he rounded the vehicle, Georgie's movements were as rapid as his, and she barred his way, even though another shiver ran through her at his proximity.

'You're so sure I'm going to fail, aren't you? And there's only one way you could be so sure, because you intend to jeopardise my work. Are you really prepared to stoop to that, just because, for some reason, you despise women?'

She felt the elation, the false courage of battle, drain from her as he did not even deign to reply to her challenge, but instead turned and dragged her suitcase from the jeep, then preceded her up the steps to the bungalow. Conscious of a sudden weariness, Georgie followed more slowly. She felt uncertain of her ground now. Almost it would have been preferable if he'd taken up the gauntlet, confirmed her suspicions. His silence left her feeling undignified, shrewish.

Niklaas's home had no charisma. It could have been any modern brick-built, single-storey bungalow, transported from suburbia to this exotic setting. Inside there was nothing to alter this first impression. The small rooms were badly in need of decoration. Very ordinary floral curtains hung at the windows. A bookcase with books stacked anyhow spilled its contents over the floor. Shabby armchairs, their chintz drearily faded, were devoid of cushions.

The tour of the bungalow didn't take long. There were two bedrooms, one Niklaas's, into which Georgie peered briefly, the other a single.

'This is yours, until such time as de Vries makes other arrangements.' So that was what he'd meant by 'temporarily'. Georgie felt even worse about her outburst.

The rest of the accommodation consisted of a living-room, kitchen and bathroom, the latter with a cheap, plastic curtain round the shower. Electricity was provided by the bungalow's own generator, housed in an outbuilding.

Looking round, unconsciously Georgie wrinkled her nose. While it was by no means filthy, the whole place had a neglected, unloved atmosphere. Whatever Niklaas did with his spare time, he certainly didn't expend it on improving his creature comforts. He had observed her reactions.

'I'm not going to apologise for this place. It suits me well enough. It doesn't measure up to Dirk's home, of course, as no doubt you'll soon discover.'

So some employees met the de Vrieses socially. After Niklaas's remark, Georgie had wondered. Dirk hadn't seemed the kind of man to draw distinctions between himself and his staff. His whole attitude after confirming her appointment had been friendly, if a little too attentive for Georgie's liking.

'Well, that's it,' said Niklaas, as they returned to the living quarters. 'If you think it worth while making any alterations to your room, feel free, but I'd rather you didn't let your enthusiasm overflow to the rest of the place. I'm not accustomed to female clutter.' This final remark led Georgie to reflect that he and his wife must have been apart for some time, for there was no evidence whatsoever that any woman had ever lived here.

'I presume you won't object,' she said with sugar-sweet politeness, 'if I flick a duster around occasionally?' She ran a finger over the folding dining-table beneath the window and held out the result for his inspection. He merely shrugged.

'As you wish. It doesn't bother me. This is just a place to sleep.'

'And eat?' she enquired.

'No. When I have time, I eat in the staff dining-room. Unfortunately the laws of nature demand an occasional intake of food, but the preparation is a damned nuisance.'

No wonder his large frame wasn't overburdened with flesh, Georgie thought, experiencing an unexpected pang of sympathy for this touchy man. With no wife to look after him he probably half starved himself. Her stepfather had shown just the same immersion in his work, but he'd had her mother to coax him away from it, to see that he ate regular meals.

'I could cook sometimes,' she said gruffly, 'if you like, and,' so that he wouldn't think she was weakening in her claim to equality, 'you can clear away and wash up.'

Niklaas hunched his shoulders in a gesture half irritation, half reluctant amusement.

'It's started! That's just one of the drawbacks of having women about—they nag!'

Georgie never slept too well the first night in a

strange bed, and she had plenty of time to consider her new situation and the man who was to be her colleague. She had been rather fortunate in one way, she considered, in that he was as distrustful, for some reason, of women as she was of men. At least in that way their relationship would be purely professional. She would have no need to fear the advances which fellow-students had made. There would be none of the consequent resentment over her rejection of them, their insinuations that she was unnatural.

It had been unlucky chance, her parents had insisted many times since, that on the one and only occasion when Georgie had imagined herself to be in love, her trust had been misplaced. At sixteen, Georgie had been an idealist, love to her a romantic, almost spiritual concept.

'You mustn't judge every man by Ralph,' her mother had told her. 'The majority of men are decent. If a girl makes her feelings on the subject of sex before marriage quite clear, nine out of ten will respect her for it.'

It might have been like that for her mother's generation, but standards were different nowadays. Georgie *had* made her feelings quite clear. Only Ralph had turned nasty. He was a strong, heavily built young man, easily able to overcome the slight teenager. She would never forget the horrible expression on his flushed face, the greedy eyes, the harsh excitement of his breathing, the groping, desecrating hands, the ultimate degradation, the screams that she had realised were her own.

She had arrived home in a state of wild hysteria, calmed only by a sedative, administered by the hastily summoned doctor. But that had not been the end of it. The resulting trauma had gone on and on. Her stepfather had been beside himself with grief and rage. Unreasonably, he felt he had failed Georgie somehow. Though she was not his own flesh and blood he had always treated her as if she were his own child. In the first flush of his anger he had been all for calling the police, but the very idea had aggravated Georgie's disturbed emotional state.

Though Maggie Jonson had been as upset as her husband, she had supported Georgie.

'The court hearing, all the unpleasantness, would be too much for her, having to relive all the details would be like experiencing them all over again. Besides, they might not believe her. Ralph isn't going to *admit* to what he did. He'll probably claim that he merely seduced her, that she wasn't unwilling.'

'But we can't let the little swine get off scot free!'

'He'd probably get away with it anyway,' Maggie said wearily. 'Rape's treated far more leniently by the courts these days. It's the old "male dominance, female submissiveness" story. There are still people who believe in it.'

In one sense Georgie had been lucky. Ralph had not made her pregnant, but the effect of his actions was long-lasting. For months there had been panic, sheer blinding, immobilising terror of all men except Paul. There had been fear, followed by fear of the fear itself, so that Georgie had done anything to avoid triggering another attack. She had become a virtual recluse, until, in sheer desperation, her parents had pleaded with her to see a psychiatrist, a female one, since Georgie would have placed no faith in a man.

To everyone's relief the treatment had been a success, and by the time she was eighteen Georgie had been secure enough to mix in male society, to attend veterinary college, and gradually the fear had lessened, self-confidence increased in her ability to work in the world of men on an equal footing. But there were no more boy-friends. Still inclined to be idealistic, Georgie felt that Ralph had destroyed that gift of inestimable value to be given to one man alone, the man she would one day love. Thus she was resolved to be not only financially independent, but also free from emotional complications. Her courage had increased so much that now, at the age of twenty-five, she was able to leave family and home to work amongst strangers, with men, with only the slightest qualm, and even this was now quieted by Niklaas's reassuring indifference.

Light was just beginning to filter through the window when Georgie woke. She was glad to be up early; she didn't want Niklaas around when she first took stock of her surroundings. She wanted to absorb the atmosphere of Marula in a spirit of calm appreciation unmarred by the conflict his presence seemed to generate.

The gentle pink sky did not last long, and by the time she gained the veranda dawn had passed into full day. The bungalow, within its protecting thorn fence, was shaded from the blazing sun by magnolias, frangipani, bauhinias, and stood on a small eminence commanding a wide-ranging view of the parkland. It was a pretty park, at least this part was, with flowering trees, flamboyants and mimosa, the ground broken up into hills and valleys.

Full of early morning energy and enthusiasm, Georgie's fit young body craved more exercise than that afforded by the confines of the veranda. She crossed the space between bungalow and thorn thicket and peered through the tall gate. The prospect before her seemed completely open, with no cover where any animal might be lurking, and she opened the gate and stepped outside, taking a deep breath of satisfaction, staring up with wonder at the blue morning-fresh bowl of the sky. Strange how it seemed to take up so much more space in this wide open landscape.

Rounding the corner of the thorn barrier, Georgie froze. Here there was an unsuspected area of long grass, and a restless quivering among the dry fronds told her she had been foolish.

A leopard had been crouching there, and now he rose to stand glaring at her. Even at this moment of mouth-drying fear, Georgie was able to appreciate the sleek beauty of his appearance, the darkly rosetted pelt, the enormous green-gold eyes. Then, with a growl, he bounded out of the grass, covering half the distance between them in a single leap.

Her first instinct was to turn and run for the gate, but she knew that to do so would be fatal. The cardinal rule was to stand her ground, but did the *leopard* know that?

CHAPTER THREE

'STAY where you are!' The voice, clipped, controlled, came from behind the fence. Niklaas had emerged silently from the bungalow. 'Keep looking at him, straight in the eye, and start to move back . . . slowly!'

The leopard's tail was lashing from side to side as he half-crouched in front of her. Slowly, frustratingly slowly, Georgie edged backwards, trying not to blink as she met the unwavering stare. After what seemed like hours her back was against the gate, and as Niklaas opened it she almost fell, saved only by an iron hand on her upper arm, dragging her to safety.

'It's a damned good job he wasn't hungry,' was his only comment.

'How can you joke about it?' Reaction had set in, and Georgie was shaking from head to toe. She wondered if she could reach the bungalow without making a fool of herself.

The problem was solved for her. Slinging his rifle, which she had not previously noticed, over one shoulder, Niklaas swung her off the floor and carried her up the steps on to the veranda, dumping her unceremoniously on to a cane lounger.

'I wasn't joking! Hungry or not, leopards are unpredictable beasts. Sometimes they'll kill just for the hell of it. Stay there!' He disappeared indoors.

Not even the contrary pride that surged in her at his authoritative tone could have got Georgie to her feet just then. Apart from the severe shock she had received, she felt very apprehensive about what was going to happen next. Almost certainly she was going to receive a harangue that would make her feel about the size of one of her almond-shaped fingernails, and she wasn't sure she could take it right now. Grimly she took a deep breath, concentrating on steadying her trembling lips.

But Niklaas's expression was inscrutable when he returned, a glass in his hand, which he held to her lips, supporting her head with his free hand.

'Drink this!'

She didn't rebel at his command but meekly downed the contents of the glass. Ugh—brandy! To Georgie, a non-drinker, it tasted foul. But within a few minutes she was experiencing its steadying effects. She looked now at the rifle where Niklaas had leant it against one of the veranda uprights.

'You ... you would have *shot* him?'

'Only if I'd had to.' His mouth was a grim line. 'I detest unnecessary waste of life.'

The leopard's or hers? She dared not ask, but she could appreciate his reluctance to destroy so magnificent a beast. Probably the fact that it hadn't been necessary was what had saved her from a lecture, for even to herself she couldn't pretend she didn't deserve censure.

'You'd better grab some breakfast.' He interrupted her thoughts.

Georgie stood up, surprised but pleased to find that her nerves were now quite steady.

'What about you?'

'I never eat breakfast. A cup of coffee will do me.'

Relief at her unexpected reprieve had made her light-headed, or perhaps it was the brandy.

'No wonder you're such a cranky person,' she said pertly. '*I* believe in going to work on a good breakfast.'

She didn't make it to the kitchen. Two large hands took her by the shoulders, swung her round, administered a shaking.

'Listen to me, smartie! So you have a sense of humour? Fine, so have I, within reason, but don't push me too far. If you hadn't been a woman, suffering from shock, and a complete Johnny raw to this country, I'd have been tempted to tan your hide for that exhibition of crass stupidity. As you pointed out yourself, Georgie, this isn't a zoo!'

Her head drooped. Every time her spirits rose in renewed optimism, he had this uncanny knack of completely demolishing her.

'I . . . I know. And I'm sorry, I didn't think.'

Firm fingers lifted a chin that had developed an annoying tendency to tremble, forcing her eyes to meet green ones which held amused exasperation.

'You're forgiven. This time.'

Georgie twisted her head from side to side, not in protest, but in bewilderment. She ought to dislike Niklaas. But her reactions just weren't that uncomplicated. One moment she could almost hate him, the next he was completely disarming, and he'd just done it again, turned on that effortless charm, to him a hollow pretence since he didn't even like her, but one which had its desired effect upon its victim.

'You've got ten minutes to get your breakfast and my coffee,' he recalled her wandering thoughts. 'If you're not ready by then I'll have to leave without you and you'll have to sit here all day twiddling your thumbs,' his teasing voice changed suddenly to bitterness, 'as my unlamented wife used to,'

Georgie wasted at least five of her precious ten minutes. Niklaas's wife was dead. 'Unlamented,' he'd said. And the *disillusion* in his voice as he'd said it! But this wasn't the only cause for her distraction. It had just occurred to her that in the past ten minutes Niklaas had carried her, touched her several times, and she had not, as usual, flinched away in distaste. In fact, now she had time to think about it, she realised she'd experienced some new, startling and very disturbing sensations which she couldn't dismiss as she would like to.

Only the sound of equipment being tossed into the rear of the jeep snapped her back to a realisation of passing time. Toast would have to do instead of the full-scale breakfast to which she'd looked forward. Hurriedly she inserted two pieces of rather dry bread into the toaster. How often and where did Niklaas shop? she wondered ruefully.

While she waited for the toast she made his coffee. How did he like it? Most men seemed to prefer it black, strong and sweet. So Georgie put in two generous spoonfuls of coffee and sugar, poured in boiling water. As she carried the tray outside on to the veranda, Niklaas was coming up the steps. He raised his eyebrows.

'It took you ten minutes to prepare *that*? It's a good job we won't be eating here!'

Georgie exercised exaggerated care as she put the tray down on to a bamboo table, because she had an idea Niklaas was expecting her to bang it down. She handed him his coffee, then stared out over the surrounding landscape as she began her meagre breakfast. Despite this morning's experience, it had lost none of its charm for her. Once more her spirits rose. She was going to love Africa, love Marula; she *knew* it. Niklaas's snort of disgust brought her head round with a snap, just in time to see the contents of his cup cascade over the edge of the veranda.

'Now what's wrong?' she demanded indignantly. 'Don't you like it?'

'Obviously not.' His eyes narrowed speculatively. 'If I thought for one minute that you'd done that on purpose . . .! Ah well, when de Vries gets back I suppose I won't have to suffer your ministrations.'

'Oh?' Perplexed, Georgie stared at him.

'Well, obviously you can't stay on here. You don't like this situation any more than I do.'

'Oh . . . oh no,' Georgie agreed hastily. Inwardly she wasn't so sure. At first she had been dismayed at the thought of sharing Niklaas's bungalow, but she wasn't afraid of him any more, and at the thought of being moved to other accommodation, possibly to live alone, she was surprised to find her reaction one of reluctance.

And, to be honest with herself at least, it wasn't just the thought of lonelinesss. Now that she knew she could trust him, she could admit that she found Niklaas unreasonably fascinating. The last forty-eight hours had been illuminating. There had been times when she had felt that his remoteness was only a façade, that a much more complex man lay beneath the surface, a man who could be kind, a man whose sense of humour he had not quite managed to submerge. As she had told him, she enjoyed a challenge, and he presented one. Could she make him like her, treat her with the respect he would have accorded to a male colleague?

'Finished?' He interrupted her musing. 'Got your equipment?'

By the time Georgie had collected her veterinary

bag from her room, Niklaas had the jeep standing outside the gate, engine revving, his fingers tapping impatiently on the steering-wheel.

'Where are we going?' she asked.

'Coincidentally, to see a leopard.' She felt rather than saw his mocking, sideways look.

'Oh.' She turned to him calmly. Leopards weren't exactly her favourite species just at this moment, but if he was expecting her to show hysterical reluctance . . .

'That's right.' His grin was definitely provoking this time. 'I do hope you won't regret the breakfast you insisted on. We have to remove his eye.' A swift, searching glance for any recoil on her part. 'It won't be a pleasant experience.'

'Operations rarely are.' Georgie was unruffled. She'd assisted her stepfather many times, and knew she wasn't squeamish.

The sick bay area was four miles away, situated within a village occupied entirely, Niklaas told her, by a contingent of the park's staff.

'A staff encampment?' Georgie queried. 'But if you didn't want me at your bungalow, why on earth didn't you take me there?'

A deep chuckle rumbled in his chest.

'You wouldn't have thanked me. Apart from language problems, I doubt you'd have been made very welcome. They're a rather self-contained community.'

'You mean *they* don't like women either?' Georgie asked with heavy irony. 'It must be a type Marula breeds.' But she felt extremely foolish a few moments later, when she discovered that the 'staff' was composed of a tribe of the indigenous peoples of the area, short, yellow-skinned, with flat, Asiaticlooking faces. Niklaas could have told her, she thought, instead of stringing her along. He had a sense of humour all right, but it was a decidedly warped one.

'Not quite what you expected?' Niklaas seemed to be enjoying his joke. 'They're related to the Hottentots, but they have their own dialect.' He proceeded to demonstrate his own fluency in this language by communicating with Mugongo, one of the game guards, in what sounded to Georgie like nothing so much as a succession of soft-sounding, subtle clicks.

'An interesting race,' he told her. 'They act as labourers, trackers and game-guards for the park, but they also have a unique culture and could, if they had to, live entirely off the land. They know which plants are edible and even how to make a kind of tea from certain shrubs. I promise you,' he added with a dry smile, 'it tastes a darn sight better than your coffee!'

'I thought we came here to see a sick animal,' she reminded him a trifle tartly. Was it just Niklaas's brand of humour, or was he deliberately trying to goad her into a show of annoyance? Could he be so against her appointment that he would manufacture a conflict as an excuse to have her dismissed when the de Vrieses returned home? Oh well, at least he wasn't a smooth seducer, she thought philosophically.

'Doesn't Dirk employ any other white staff?' she asked, as Mugongo led them towards a far enclosure.

'Yes. There's another village, not far from the entrance to the park, a mixture of English and Afrikaaners. They're mostly connected with the tourist side of things—guides, car mechanics, a few scientists. De Vries will probably fix you up there, if I ask him to.'

And Georgie had no doubt that he would ask. Very much the loner, Niklaas would prefer to have his bungalow to himself.

They were standing outside their patient's pen by now, and Niklaas was already assessing the young leopard's uneasy behaviour, as it paced the pen, uttering low, menacing growls.

'Look at that eye, that's our problem.'

'Not a pretty sight,' Georgie agreed, professionalism taking over from personal considerations. The eye was swollen and clotted with blood, the cornea distended and bulging. 'Will you dart him?'

'Yes, unless of course you have a yen to try your hand at leopard taming again?'

Why was it that even his mildest tongue-in-cheek remarks tempted her to inflict physical damage on him? She'd always had a quick temper, but surely she'd never found it this difficult to contain? She forced back a pithy retort and watched intently as Niklaas prepared to fire the projectile syringe.

'How did it happen?' she asked, filled with distress at the disfiguration, the beautiful animal's obvious discomfort.

'Who knows? A fight, a sharp thorn?'

'And removal is the only way?'

'Do you think I'd be operating if it weren't? There's a risk of the other eye becoming infected if I leave it any longer.'

'Will he survive in the wild with only one eye?'

'I believe so. Animals are very adaptable, though de Vries and his mother would have you believe differently.'

'Dirk?' Georgie was surprised. 'He doesn't think you should operate?'

'His contention is that it's only one animal, that the operation, the after-care needed, are a waste of time and money. Reita, that's his mother, has different ideas. *She* has her eye on the skin—it's an unusually fine one. And with another seven like it . . .' Niklaas's eyes were fixed intently on the leopard as he waited for it to succumb to the drug.

A cold chill crept down Georgie's back.

'You mean Mrs de Vries would actually . . .?'

'Have a fur made up? Yes, that's dear Reita for you.'

'What on earth is someone like that doing running this sort of place?' Georgie asked furiously.

'The thought sickens you?'

'Well, naturally, doesn't it you?'

'Yes, and fortunately Reita has no say in the running of the place. She just uses it, lives here when it suits. She's what I call a commuter wife, only she's a widow now, of course. She commutes back and forth to the bright lights, Jo'burg or Cape Town. Her husband, now . . .' Niklaas's voice deepened and it was apparent to Georgie that he held the late Mr de Vries in great respect, even perhaps affection. 'Klaus was a dedicated man. Every creature on this territory was as dear to him as a member of his own family. An animal was put down only as a very last resort. He even hated it when we had to deal with a man-eating lion, or rogue elephant.'

'And does Dirk feel the same way?'

'Don't you know?'

'Of course I don't. I keep telling you, I hardly know him.'

'Oh.' He still sounded disbelieving, but he answered her question. 'Dirk has no strong feelings one way or the other. He inherited Marula, but he's not the outdoor type. To do him more justice than he deserves, it's not his fault. He just hasn't the constitution for it. He's been sickly in one way or another since childhood. I don't know exactly what's wrong with him—I'm not sure he does. Reita tends to treat him as if he were still in short trousers'.

This seemed to dispose of Niklaas's interest in their employer, and he turned away to speak to the game guard, words and gestures indicating that Mugongo and some of his fellows should carry the leopard into the operating theatre, a long, low, concrete building adjoining the sick pens.

'Perhaps that's why Dirk's never married,' Georgie pursued the theme as they followed their patient. 'No one in their right mind would fancy a possessive mother-in-law.'

'Oh, I don't know. Some women might consider it worth the risk to snare a rich husband.'

The surgery was well equipped, and, snapping back into her professional role, Georgie quickly took in its layout. Without waiting to be asked, she began to lay out cloths and the familiar, sterilised instruments in the order in which they would be required, while Niklaas cleansed the wound site with surgical soap and shaved the surrounding area.

Silent, all other considerations forgotten in their concentration on the coming task, they scrubbed up. Scalpel in hand, ready to make the first incision, Niklaas paused, giving Georgie a quizzical glance.

'Sure you're not squeamish?' he probed. 'Not likely to faint? Because, if you do, you'll lie where you fall. Once I start this job, it will need all my concentration.'

'Naturally,' Georgie answered calmly. 'I've assisted at dozens of operations. Let's get on with it, shall we?'

Carefully he incised the skin on each side of the eyelashes, so that the conjunctiva would be removed with the eyeball. Georgie found her eyes hypnotically drawn to the delicately moving hands—so large, she marvelled, yet so skilful and gentle.

Deftly, Niklaas was separating the eye from its surrounding muscles, and automatically Georgie's hand moved to pass him the long, curved forceps which would clamp the eyestalk, preventing bleeding, her reward his approving 'Good girl!' Such a minor concession, yet she found herself glowing with pleasure.

As he worked, it was also her task to watch the patient's respiration and general condition, alert for any signs of collapse. But all seemed to be going well. The ligatures were in place and secured, and Niklaas could now remove the actual eye.

'Would you like to do the final suturing?' he asked, surprising her.

Georgie nodded, and when her line of neat stitches was almost complete she packed the cavity with antibiotic solution, sutured a pad over the wound as added protection, and treated the surrounding skin surface with antiseptic. About five minutes later the leopard began to show signs of recovery, and was carried back to his enclosure. Side by side, Niklaas and Georgie watched his first tentative movements.

'The operation was a success, but we still have the

after-care period to get through.' Niklaas didn't sound worried, in fact his tone was jubilant, and to Georgie's amazement, he had thrown a casual arm across her shoulders.

'You told the truth, Georgie Jonson. You'll make a damned good vet!'

Georgie swallowed convulsively, eyes pricking. Of course, he might have made the same gesture to any colleague, after successful surgery—he was probably unaware of his compulsive gesture. But unawareness was not the reaction Georgie experienced. Oh God, she thought, as if their professional relationship wasn't tricky enough, however much she resisted she couldn't help being aware of Niklaas as a man. She moved away, saying lightly:

'Even your compliments have reservations, don't they? May I remind you, I already *am* a vet.'

'Mmm, but still with a long way to go!' His words could be as sharp as his scalpel, yet before she could turn on him with a protest, he was continuing as if he hadn't just deliberately shot her down. 'Care to see more of the parkland after lunch?' He had moved up behind her, so close that his breath fanned her cheek, so close that she could feel the warmth emanating from him, smell an unmistakably masculine odour that was not unpleasant. She started convulsively, the movement causing her thigh to brush his.

'Yes—yes, I would.' Georgie's heart had suddenly begun to pound in her throat, and she tried to make her unsteady voice sound like breathless eagerness. What on earth was wrong with her today? She asked herself crossly. Thank goodness Niklaas appeared not to notice her confusion.

'We won't be able to cover the whole park in one

go, of course. Mugongo and his team make daily
tours, looking for sick or wounded animals, and I
try to inspect a different area each day. But with
surgery work to be done, it takes me a full week to
work from one end to the other.'

Lunch was a hasty meal. Niklaas obviously didn't
believe in wasting time over the social niceties.
Reluctantly he paused long enough to introduce
Georgie to other members of staff, who were using
the clinically functional canteen. They were all
men, Georgie noted, and when she commented
Niklaas told her:

'Only a couple of the older men have wives and
families on the park. Marula seems to jinx
marriages.'

The tour of inspection was full of the incident for
which Georgie had previously hoped. In the lower
lying areas they saw eland and waterbuck, a pride of
lions drowsing in the shade of an acacia thicket.
Elephants paused in their browsing and solemnly
regarded the jeep's passage. But the sight Georgie
found most appealing was that of giraffe, cantering
rocking-horse style, their long necks swaying
dreamily in a curiously elegant gangliness.

'Oh,' she breathed, turning impulsively to the
man at her side, 'I feel so lucky, so privileged to be
actually working and living somewhere like this!'

'Hmm,' Niklaas looked at her curiously, 'I
believe you mean it, or at least,' he qualified, 'you
think you mean it.'

'I know whether I mean something or not!'
Georgie snapped. His scepticiscm was becoming a
little wearing.

Feeling snubbed and slightly hurt, for despite the

occasional taunt he had been almost friendly today, Georgie subsided, and thereafter concentrated on appreciating the spectacle of the park's wildlife without any further voicing of her enjoyment.

They ate before returning to the bungalow. It had been a long, hot day, and when Niklaas offered Georgie first use of the shower, she accepted gladly. The cold sting of the water was reviving, and she felt the tiredness drain from her body, an uplifting euphoria replacing fatigue, as she reviewed her first full working day at Marula. She felt she had acquitted herself well, given Niklaas no cause for complaint, and as for his qualities as a colleague, she felt she could have been far less fortunate.

As she towelled herself dry, she caught a glimpse of herself in the full-length mirror, and for the first time in a long while she paused to study her reflection, something which she usually avoided. She hadn't a bad figure, she acknowledged now. She knew she could have made more of it than she did, but the boyish, unflattering jeans and shirts she affected most of the time were deliberate camouflage.

She pulled her robe round her, and gathering up an armful of discarded clothes, her towel and sponge bag, left the bathroom, encountering Niklaas on the threshold.

'Oh, good, you've finished!' His tone was matter-of-fact, but Georgie started perceptibly. She dropped her possessions as, with one hand, she clutched unnecessarily at the front of her robe.

Without any comment, Niklaas stooped to help her, just as Georgie herself crouched down. Their foreheads met with some force, and before Georgie could save herself she toppled sideways. The long arm that shot out, steadying her, pulling her to her feet, also brushed against the soft swell of her breast, its outline clearly defined through the material of her robe. She heard Niklaas catch his breath, knew that her own panicky gasp had been audible. For a moment lost from time they stared at each other, before, with a little cry of protest, Georgie tore herself free and ran for her room, abandoning her belongings. Inside the door, she rested against it for an instant, needing its support, heard Niklaas's footsteps just outside and began to tremble violently.

'Your things are outside your door,' she heard him say, his voice hard, cold.

It was some time before she dared to retrieve them, but when she did there was no sign of Niklaas, just the jetting sound of the shower across the hallway.

She must remember, Georgie told herself, as slowly her nerves settled, she wasn't at home. It was insufficient to move from bathroom to bedroom clad as she was now. In future she would take fresh clothes in with her and dress fully before emerging. She'd been lucky this time. Niklaas had been annoyed by her carelessness, but if he'd been any other man . . . She shuddered again, knowing that, woman-hater or not, he had reacted to that accidental contact, an accident that must not be allowed to occur again.

CHAPTER FOUR

'WHY the haversack, and why the change of clothes?' Georgie asked next morning, as she hurled herself into the jeep, where Niklaas already waited, tense and impatient to be gone. His crisp commands had been issued from outside her bedroom door only ten minutes ago. He hadn't given her a chance for even the scantiest breakfast this morning. But recognising the urgency in his tone, Georgie had decided not to quibble.

To her relief he made absolutely no reference to the previous evening, and as the jeep bumped over the uneven ground behind the bungalow, in the opposite direction to the surgery, she decided he would be as anxious as she was to forget the incident.

'Because we may have to be out all day and all night.'

'Where are we going?'

'To the farthest limits of the park, where it adjoins the next property. We've had a report that one of our elephants has gone rogue, killed an African.'

'But that means . . .'

'I'll have to kill it.'

'What makes an elephant turn rogue?' Georgie asked.

'Could be one of a number of things.' Niklaas didn't sound in the mood to inform, but Georgie persisted.

'Such as?'

'Toothache, or other kinds of pain. Provocation.
A bull will always defend his herd. Occasionally a
female separated from her young will charge. As a
rule they don't normally attack humans—their urge
is to escape. But if they've been hunted or wounded,
then they're dangerous.' His speech was unusually
terse and clipped, and Georgie suspected that, like
the late Klaus de Vries, Niklaas was reluctant to
end an animal's life.

They were a long way now from the wide open
areas that surrounded Niklaas's bungalow. It was
Georgie's first experience of driving through the
actual bush, and to her untutored eyes there seemed
to be no trail at all. It was as if Niklaas plunged the
vehicle straight at impenetrable growth, and several times she had to restrain herself from
flinching, as low-hanging vegetation brushed the
windows and canvas canopy.

It was almost dusk when they reached the
boundaries of Marula and were greeted by local
Africans, one of whom led them to where the rogue
elephant had last been seen. Not only that, but he
insisted on showing them the actual spot where the
elephant had killed the man. Just a few pitiful
tattered rags and deep holes where the animal had
rammed his tusks into the ground showed that a
man had lived and was now dead.

'It's too dark to do anything tonight.' Niklaas
communicated his decision to the African, who,
after much shrugging and protesting, led them back
the way they'd come. 'We'll make camp and
continue the search at first light.'

'Make camp?' Georgie looked around her. There
was no native village here.

'Yes—and don't worry! I've brought *two* tents!'

For Georgie, sleeping under canvas was no novelty, but this was a very special experience. It was also a misnomer. Sleep was slow in coming, for her excitement, her sense of adventure, were mingled with apprehension about tomorrow. There was a feeling of strangeness, too, about sleeping in the open in a strange country, only inches away from a man she hardly knew. For though the tents were separate, they were pitched close together and Georgie could hear his slightest movement. They talked desultorily for a while, Niklaas interpreting for her the increasing chorus of night sounds, the cough of a leopard, a night bird brushing past on rushing wings, the snarls and whoops of the prowling hyenas.

'According to the Africans, hyenas are the spirits of the dead. They believe that old men who die have the power to come back as hyenas.'

Georgie shivered. She wasn't superstitious, though as a child she had experienced similar delicious frissons of fear during the telling of ghost stories, in which she did not believe yet could not wholly dismiss, and by night, in this strange setting, it was almost possible to credit such legends.

'Am I scaring you?' asked Niklaas.

'No, of course not. But I am a bit worried about tomorrow,' she confessed. 'Are you?'

'Why should I be?' There was amusement in his tone.

'Well, I suppose there's bound to be some danger. You could get hurt?'

There was a long, deep silence. Then, sounding oddly intent:

'And that worries you?'

'A little.'

'Why should it?' Then, speculatively, 'Afraid you might have to find your own way back, if I get killed?'

'No!' Georgie was sharply indignant. Trust him to misunderstand. She wished she hadn't even mentioned the subject.

'Why else should you have any concern for me?'

'I'd be concerned for anyone in the same situation,' she asserted.

But another silence followed, and as, presently, the sound of Niklaas's regular breathing told her he slept, she knew that wasn't quite true. Niklaas could never be just anyone. He was most uniquely himself. Nor did he fit her preconceived ideas, instilled by Dirk, ideas which had dictated her attitude towards him. But that had undergone a subtle alteration. He could still annoy her, deliberately she suspected, but she had only respect for his professionalism, his dedication to his work, and between annoyance and respect lay a complexity of emotions she could not analyse.

Their African guide was prompt next morning. Understandably so, Georgie supposed. He would be anxious to have Niklaas deal with the threat to his tribe.

They saw plenty of elephants, a herd on the move, that included many babies, determinedly imitating their mothers' movements, flapping their ears and keeping pace with the cows whenever they moved on. But there was no sign of any enraged bull, though the foremost elephant, a huge matriarch, had her ears fanned out, her trunk stretched directly and rigidly in their direction.

'Just a protective bluff,' Niklaas assured Georgie. 'Besides, I wouldn't expect an animal that's gone rogue to be with the herd. They're usually loners, outcasts, often an old bull that's been ousted from his leadership by a younger male. I believe animals are as capable as humans of suffering from rejection.' There was a note in his voice that made Georgie suspect that this was a bitter, if unintentional, reference to the failure of his marriage.

'There's not much cover here for an elephant,' she pointed out, and indeed the trees in the area were scattered wide apart, the elephants standing in the open for anyone to see.

'No.' As swiftly as he had dropped into reflective mood, Niklaas cast it aside. 'And I reckon the fellow we're after will have made for cover. Amazing creatures, elephants. Even though he may have gone berserk, some spark of intelligence will still remain, warning him to lie low, avoid retribution.'

After driving for some considerable distance, with many stops for their guide to examine the ground, they came to an area where the vegetation was more dense, the elephant grass as high as a man's shoulder. As the vehicle slowed, the African jumped down, and as usual began casting about for spoor signs, like a working terrier on the trail of game. A moment or two later his urgently beckoning hand told them he had found what he sought, and Niklaas translated his swift, excited chatter.

'He says it's the same beast.'

'How can he possibly be certain?' queried Georgie.

'Size of tracks, shape. These fellows can tell one

animal from another in the way a policeman reads fingerprints. Hmm, a big fellow by the look of it. Georgie,' decisively, 'you'll stay in the jeep.'

'I most certainly won't!' she asserted immediately. 'I'm coming with you.' She was filled with an odd certainty that just so long as Niklaas was within her sight nothing could happen to him.

'Georgie, I'm going to need all my concentration. I don't want the added worry of having to protect you.'

'Then *don't* worry. I'm another vet. I'm coming with you and there's no way you can stop me. Besides, you might be glad of some back-up support.'

He looked at the second rifle which Georgie had snatched up.

'You?' he mocked. 'Back-up support? With that? It's nearly as big as you are! You're more likely to blow your own brains out, or shoot me in the back.'

'Much as I should love to do that,' she said with sarcastic sweetness, 'I promise you there's no danger of my doing it accidentally. I'm an excellent shot.'

'Damn it, Georgie, do you want to be trampled to death? Get back in the jeep, we're wasting time.'

But Georgie followed in his wake, for she was beginning to suspect that, despite his cold, impenetrable manner, he had his own form of vulnerability.

'Back home,' Georgie told him, 'during the last foxhunting season, my stepfather was off sick and I had to put down no fewer than six injured hunters, even though I love horses.'

'All right, so you're a hard woman, but you don't put down horses with an elephant gun.'

'True, but I *can* handle it. You were complaining,' she reminded him, 'about wasting time.' She gestured towards the African, already some yards ahead, and looking back anxiously for them to follow.

In single file, they followed the African, trying to avoid making any noise that might break the absolute stillness and give away their presence. From their guide's gestures, Georgie guessed that the elephant was close, yet uncannily there was no sound. The tension of the still atmosphere communicated itself to her, and niggling fears for Niklaas's safety rose again to torment her. She gripped the rifle tightly in sweating hands.

The trail led to the environs of a waterhole, and here Niklaas took command, signalling the African to retreat. With unexpected suddenness, a large grey head appeared above the edge of the hole, less than thirty yards from where they stood. Georgie caught her breath. If his body matched the size of that head, he was enormous.

Up went the bull's trunk. Despite the care they had exercised, the wind, freakishly, had changed direction, and he had discovered their presence. The grey giant heaved himself on to dry land. He was big all right, and he was advancing towards them.

'Get back, Georgie, well back!' Niklaas muttered. 'If this is our fellow, he may charge at any moment, and it'll be fast. An elephant is capable of fifteen miles an hour over a short distance.'

Now was not the time to argue, but Georgie had no intention of retreating altogether as their guide had done. Safety catch off, rifle at the ready, she moved slowly backwards, her eyes never leaving the tusker.

The animal advanced again, stopped, ears flapping slowly forward. Up went his trunk again, and he began to rock from foot to foot with increasing intensity, a movement that Georgie knew heralded the charge. Then he was moving, at incredible speed, trunk doubled back behind his tusks, his incongruously little mouth issuing screams and snorts of hatred and rage.

Niklaas took careful aim and fired. There was no doubt that the shot had found its target, yet it seemed not to have affected the giant's steamroller approach. About to fire again, stepping backwards to keep distance between himself and the creature, Niklaas caught his foot in a root and fell, sprawled in the advancing animal's path. He lay frighteningly still.

But there was no time to indulge fear. Georgie lifted her rifle and, with a prayer on her lips, fired. As the enormous recoil flung her to the ground, she heard the elephant squeal his outrage. His hide must be so tough that neither Niklaas's bullet nor hers had made any impression. But as she scrambled to her feet she saw the headlong rush falter. The elephant staggered and agonisingly slowly, like the slow-motion collapse of some great demolished chimney, he began to sag, to topple, crashing finally only feet from Niklaas's recumbent body.

Georgie ran, to fall on her knees at Niklaas's side. His eyes were closed, and a thin line of blood ran from a wound on his head, where he must have struck his head against some sharp object.

'Help me get him back to the jeep,' she commanded the African. He didn't understand her words, but her tone and gestures sufficed. Between them they managed to lift the unconscious man and struggle back to the vehicle and the first-aid kit.

Ten minutes later Georgie had the relief of seeing Niklaas regain consciousness. At first he looked about him in bewilderment, and she wondered anxiously whether he could be concussed, but then his expression cleared and she saw satisfaction cross his face.

'I got him, then, or I wouldn't be here to tell the tale. What happened exactly?'

'After you fired, you stepped backwards and tripped. You knocked yourself out.' She wondered at her diplomacy.

'But the elephant went down?'

'Yes,' she confirmed. 'He went down all right.'

Niklaas sat up, stood up and issued a rapid string of instructions to the African guide.

'I've told him to fetch his people. They'll dispose of the body.'

'How?' asked Georgie.

'Dismember it, cook parts of it.' A teasing grin curved his mouth. 'Fancy staying to supper? Elephant's trunk is quite popular with connoisseurs of elephants' meat. It tastes a bit like boiled tongue.'

Georgie shuddered, shaking her head. Reaction at Niklaas's near escape was beginning to set in and she felt slightly sick, but he was laughing at her wry grimace.

'I'll go and give them a hand, while you prepare something more to your taste.'

'Will *you* be eating elephant?' she asked.

'No, it takes ten hours of boiling to get it really tender. By the time they get down to their feast I want to be well on our way home—goodness knows what emergencies will have cropped up in our absence.'

Their simple rations were ready when Niklaas returned, and Georgie looked up at his approach, ready with a cheerful greeting, but the words died on her lips at the sight of his expression. His whole body seemed visibly taut, deep lines incised his face and the green eyes were cold. Had it been the wrong elephant after all? Was that why he looked so furious? Without comment, he took the dish she handed him and gulped down its contents, though obviously without appetite.

Under long dark eyelashes, Georgie observed him anxiously. This silence was like the calm before a storm, and as the tension grew she feared the outbreak was not far distant.

Niklaas finished eating, helped her to clear away, dismantled the tents, all in the same total silence. Finally, after the jeep had travelled some distance, she could bear it no longer.

'Is something wrong? Is it your head? Would you like me to drive?'

'Oh, so you can drive, can you?' he snarled.

'Of course.' She was surprised by his ferocity.

'Georgie,' he said grimly, 'why didn't you tell me?'

'Tell you what?' she prevaricated, but she knew now what was on his mind.

'That *I* didn't kill that beast, that you did? And don't tell me it was to spare my feelings.'

Georgie was angry. A little gratitude wouldn't have come amiss. After all, she *had* saved his life!

'If you had any brains in that thick skull of yours,' she snapped, 'you'd know the answer. You don't think the elephant would have been content with trampling over you, do you? I'd have been his next target. I fired to save my own life as much as yours. How did you find out anyway?'

'Apart from the fact that Nganga was full of your praises, I do have the use of my eyes. There were two bullet wounds between that beast's eyes. I only fired once.'

Georgie's anger was always swift to fade. Now she felt miserable.

'For heaven's sake ... you had an unfortunate accident. It could have happened to anyone. If you hadn't tripped you'd have fired again, and that would have been the end of it. But you did trip. Are you trying to tell me I was wrong to fire, that I should have *let* him walk right over you, perhaps gore you, as he gored that poor African?'

She couldn't say another word. She was fighting back tears. They were tears of anger, she told herself savagely. The jeep jerked to a halt and with a sound that denoted ... exasperation? contrition ...? Niklaas turned and put his arms round her.

'Georgie, Georgie! I'm sorry. I'm an ungrateful swine. Of course you had to fire, and I'm damned glad you did. It's just that ...' Niklaas's tone had mellowed so much that she ventured to tease, peeping up at him from beneath tear-spiked lashes.

'You couldn't bring yourself to accept that a "mere woman" had saved your life. Don't worry, I won't tell any of your friends.'

He bent his head and gently brushed his lips across her forehead.

'Thank you, Georgie,' he said quietly, 'for saving my life, though I'm not sure it was worth saving. As to telling my friends,' he shrugged, 'again, I'm not sure I have any.'

'I'm not surprised,' she dared to say gently, 'if you treat everyone the way you treat me.'

'And do you consider yourself to be one of my friends?' he asked, his eyes searching hers, their blue still brilliant with the unshed tears.

She tried to meet the enigmatic green gaze steadily.

'That's all I've ever wanted, to be friendly.' Her voice held a vibrancy she could not conceal, her lips parted on a sudden unsteady breath.

Suddenly she was close in his arms, crushed against the hardness of his chest, which rose and fell violently. His hand was under her chin, forcing her head back, as his mouth took advantage of lips that had parted in surprised alarm.

'Niklaas! No, no . . .' she gasped, but he ignored her protest.

'Georgie, Georgie—dear God!' His voice was almost incoherent. It seemed he could only express his meaning in action, his kiss going on and on, bruising her lips, probing her mouth. When he finally dragged his lips from hers, it was only to move them lower, down her throat, while his hands began to move over her body, stroking, searching, caressing.

Frantically Georgie began to fight, fear spiralling, mind and body transported back to a moment almost ten years ago, which had begun like this and ended in terror. But Niklaas responded immediately, releasing her, his voice thickened but charged with anger—at her, or at himself?

'Damn it! Damn it to hell!'

She was taken by surprise as the jeep's engine jarred into life once more and the vehicle surged forward, Niklaas driving for once without regard for the stringent speed restrictions. Maltreated tyres squealed as the vehicle drew up outside the bungalow.

'Get out, Georgie!' The words came from between set lips.

'Niklaas—' she began tremulously.

'Get out.' He was staring straight ahead of him, a nerve twitching violently in his jaw.

She slid from the seat, watched as the jeep roared away, leaving her alone.

She was tired, Georgie realised, as she entered the bungalow and went to her room. It was not just physical fatigue, but a weariness of heart, of mind. She lay flat on her back, staring up at the ceiling. Was it all going to go wrong? She wondered drearily? What had started out as a new life, a great adventure, an exciting career, had suddenly become not just their original battle of wits, which could have been fun, nor just a fight for her right to equality; it had become more personal.

Niklaas, like her, avoided emotional relationships. He would be angry, not only with her, but with himself for his lowered guard. To him, that violent, brief lovemaking had been only the outcome of reaction, his near-escape from death. He couldn't know what it had done to her.

Despite these dismal thoughts, her eyelids drooped and she drifted into sleep, not noticing the sudden crossing of the borderline between day and night. She did not hear her bedroom door open and close, was oblivious of any presence, until the light snapped on and Niklaas sat heavily on the edge of her bed. She opened sleep-glazed eyes to find him staring enigmatically down at her. She caught her breath, teeth latching on to her bottom lip.

'You startled me,' she said unnecessarily. But she knew that the sudden irregularity of her heartbeat was not due merely to the fact that he had taken her unawares. She was utterly unnerved, not by his presence, but by her own reaction to it. This was not the man who had driven away tortured by a physical frustration he despised. Instead, she noted with a stir of sympathy, he looked drained of all emotion, his green eyes dulled, infinite dejection in the slump of his shoulders. A strange sensation swelled her breasts into a rapid rise and fall.

'You look tired,' she whispered.

'I am tired. Tired and fed up!' His voice was hard, yet the betraying expression in his eyes moved her unbearably. She found herself wanting to get up and go to him, to put her arms about him, to try and lift some of the burden that seemed to oppress him. Instead:

'Do you want to talk about it?' she asked, carefully casual. Niklaas would resent any show of what seemed like pity.

'Why should you be interested in my problems,' he enquired bitterly, 'especially after the way I behaved? I never intended . . . I *knew* your presence here meant trouble for me. It's a long time since I . . . Purposely I've kept away from women. Why the hell Dirk had to . . . What's he up to? Is it spite because . . .?' He looked at Georgie as if she could supply the answers to his incoherent questions.

She stretched out a tentative hand, offering it to him.

'About what happened,' she said, 'it was an impulse. You were tired, you'd just been under tremendous strain. People do foolish things. I'm willing to forget it, if you are. Can't we pretend it never happened and begin again, as friends, colleagues?'

'Is that what you want?' Niklaas sounded incredulous, and as she nodded timidly he took her hand in both of his, smiled. It was a wry, twisted effort, but at least it was a smile.

'You're a very generous person, Georgie. I promise you, nothing like that will ever occur again.'

Something inside her wrenched painfully, illogically, at the certainty in his promise, but she forced a smile. He was still holding her hand, his fingers moving in an abstractedly caressive way that sent shafts of strange sensation through her body. Gently she withdrew her hand.

'So that's all right, then? Goodnight, Niklaas.'

'Goodnight.' Halfway to the door he paused, turned, lingered, looking at her. 'I suppose you wouldn't care to join me in a nightcap?' he said abruptly. 'Somehow I don't think I shall sleep just yet.'

Georgie hesitated. To agree might be to incur further complications. But to refuse was to make a nonsense of their agreement. Besides, his drawn face tugged at her heartstrings. She sat up.

'You know I don't drink?'

'I think I can find you a tomato juice.'

'OK, then.' She swung her feet to the floor and followed him into the living-room, choosing a chair as far away from him as possible.

For himself, she noticed, he had poured a double whisky, and she frowned a little. Alcohol might reawaken physical needs. He was staring round the room, an expression of intense distaste on his face, an expression which his words presently confirmed.

'It's like a prison cell.'

'Well,' she strove for tact, 'I *have* seen more cheerful rooms.'

'It's not just the room,' he said explosively, 'it's the whole damned place. It's not a home, it's a morgue. I loathe it. It must look even worse to you, a woman?'

'It's not that bad,' Georgie said, purposely cheerful. 'I could make some improvements,' she ventured. 'But you did say,' she added hastily as he turned brooding eyes upon her, 'that you didn't like a lot of female clutter.'

'You forget,' he said, 'you won't be here much longer. You'll be getting your own accommodation.'

'Oh. Yes.' Somehow that fact had faded to the back of her mind.

'Lysette disliked this place, even when it did look like a home. No, it was more than dislike—she hated it, and in the end she hated me too. I should never have married her, brought her here, never. My life demands too much of a woman, and perhaps I'm damnably selfish, but I could never give it up. City life would stifle me.' He fell silent over his drink.

Georgie waited quietly.

'Lysette was like a fish out of water.'

'If she loved you it shouldn't have mattered,' Georgie said with quiet conviction. It was none of her business, yet she felt a spurt of resentment against the woman who could still make Niklaas look like this. But he was shaking his head.

'No. It was asking too much of any woman. This country is too hot, too dry. Perhaps if I'd had a home like Marula Lodge to offer her, with air-conditioning, fitted out with everything money could buy. If I'd had the money, or the inclination, for the social round. She was bored.'

'She could have taken more interest in her home,' Georgie said hotly. 'And she had you . . .' She stopped, flushing, but Niklaas didn't seem to have noticed the words which, quite unexpectedly, had slipped out.

'She wasn't accustomed to housework. I took on a couple of African servants, but she didn't like them, said they "smelled different".' Niklaas had downed his whisky and now he was pouring himself a second, even more generous than the first. Georgie parted her lips to protest, but changed her mind. If she interrupted him now, she might not hear the story out, and she found herself wanting to know everything, to understand. 'She was always saying she must have been mad to come to a place like this. The ants bothered her, the flies made her feel sick, and in the end she didn't spend much time here. She was always . . .' He stopped short, banging down his empty glass on the table. 'Well, she's gone now and I threw out everything that reminded me of her, hence the Spartan conditions. I've no need now to consult any woman's likes and dislikes. I can please myself where and how I live.' Despite his assertion, his tone of voice gave no indication of pleasure in his situation. He stood up, lurching slightly. 'I think,' he said apologetically, 'that I'm a little drunk. I don't usually . . .'

'Drunk, and tired too,' Georgie said gently. 'Why not go to bed? You'll probably sleep now.'

'Mmm, in a while. I wanted you to understand, Georgie, why I have to keep you, to keep all women, at a distance, why I'll never ask another woman to share my life here. I'm sorry if I offended you, scared you. I did scare you, didn't I?'

'We agreed to forget that,' Georgie reminded him softly.

'Thanks for listening to my drunken ramblings.' His oddly attractive smile twisted his features. 'You're a good sort, Georgie,' his voice was slurred now, the words coming with difficulty, 'yes, a good sort, not like a woman at all.'

Niklaas's final observation did not please Georgie as much as it might once have done, she realised as she prepared for bed. She was glad that he had chosen to confide in her, even though his confidences had been imparted in a mood of maudlin reminiscence, brought about by fatigue, the aftermath of the elephant hunt and a little too much whisky. Normally Niklaas would not be the type to indulge in self-pity or seek for sympathy. In fact, he would probably be furious with himself tomorrow.

And the next day, as she had expected, he was himself again, totally in control, still sarcastic on occasion. But even so, Georgie couldn't help cherishing the conviction that, whatever Niklaas thought, the incidents of the previous day had brought them a new understanding of each other, of the need of each for personal barriers.

At the end of the morning's session, Niklaas returned to the bungalow for some forgotten equipment, and Georgie took the opportunity to return too, for a shower. The weather was becoming increasingly sultry, and her clothes were sticking to her most unpleasantly.

She showered hastily, since Niklaas had warned her the break could not be a protracted one, and it was while she was drying herself that she became aware of voices raised in conflict. She dressed hastily and eased open the bathroom door.

'No! You know damn well I swore never to cross your threshold again, and you know why.' It was Niklaas, his deep voice roughened by a feeling more than just anger. 'If you want the girl, then invite her, but leave me out of it.'

Georgie moved towards her room, hoping to avoid detection. She didn't want to be discovered eavesdropping, but she must have made some slight sound, for almost immediately Niklaas emerged from the living-room.

'Georgie!' His voice held the sarcastic note she most disliked. 'Come in. There's someone here I know you're very anxious to meet again.'

It was Dirk de Vries and, surprising Georgie, for their acquaintance was so slight, he stepped forward and took her hand, but at the same time bent to brush her cheek with his lips.

'I'm sorry I wasn't here to welcome you to Marula. But I see Nik has been making you comfortable.' He turned to the other man, a sandy eyebrow quirked sardonically. 'A bit out of character for you, housing Georgie, compromising yourself?'

'And what,' snapped Niklaas, 'was I supposed to do with her? Your place was all shut up. Besides, you know it's essential I should have my assistant close at hand in case of emergencies. If she'd been the man I expected—but you were the one who was damn fool enough to hire a woman.' Then Georgie, whose heart had been sinking rapidly at his words as she saw what she thought of as their growing working rapport crumbling, heard her reprieve.

'Anyway, we've come to terms with the situation. We don't see it in any other way than that of colleagues.'

A wry smile creased Dirk de Vries's rather pallid skin.

'I can see Georgie's point, but you must be blind, old boy. However, suppose we ask Georgie for her views? Would you like me to arrange alternative accommodation?'

Four days ago Georgie would have jumped at the chance of complaining about her accommodation, of insisting on other provision. But now, slightly bewildered, she realised she would be very reluctant to move out of Niklaas's bungalow.

'Georgie?' Dirk was waiting for an answer.

'I'll be OK, Dirk. This isn't exactly five-star accommodation'—she didn't want to sound over-keen to remain, and foster the wrong impression in either man—'but it's adequate.' She ignored Niklaas's interjected, sarcastic 'thank you very much'. 'And, as Niklaas said, it is more convenient in an emergency.'

Dirk shrugged goodnaturedly.

'Just as you like. You're over twenty-one, both of you.' Then, 'Sure you won't change your mind about that dinner tonight, Nik? My mother's anxious to meet Georgie.'

'Look her over, you mean!' Niklaas retorted. 'Georgie must please herself. Just get her back in reasonable time. Our work calls for us to be larks, not night owls like you and Reita. As for me,' his burnished head moved from side to side, 'count me out.' His manner towards his employer was scarcely conciliatory, Georgie thought.

'How about it, then?' Dirk was looking at her, his

expression eager, as if her decision were really important to him. 'Dinner tonight, up at Marula Lodge?'

Georgie couldn't see any reason why Niklaas should object, and besides, she was curious about the de Vrieses, mother and son. She accepted.

'Good-oh! I'll pick you up at six. *Tot siens*!'

After a full afternoon in the surgery, Georgie didn't feel much like making the effort to dress up and go socialising, but Niklaas's astute comment to that effect stiffened her spine and her resolution.

'I'm not in the least tired, and I'm simply dying to see Dirk's house and meet his mother.'

'Hmph!' Niklaas's snort was untranslatable.

Unaware that she would be quite so far from civilisation, Maggie Jonson had insisted that her daughter should pack several dresses in the bulk of her luggage which had now arrived. Georgie pondered over what to wear. Did Dirk and his mother dress formally for dinner? She wouldn't have thought so, not just to entertain a mere employee, but even so jeans and shirt would scarcely be *de rigueur*.

Finally she decided on a cocktail-length dress in a powder-blue which pointed up the silvery fairness of her wavy hair and clung enticingly about her slender figure. Matching shoes completed the outfit, and gave her more confidence when she emerged from her room and encountered Niklaas. She was able now, by virtue of her high heels, to meet his gaze more directly, finding that she was hoping for just a few words that might be construed as a compliment.

The glint of something indefinable in his green

eyes was so quickly banished that Georgie could not be certain she'd seen it, let alone interpreted its meaning, but there was no doubt about the construction to be placed on his words.

'Doing Dirk proud, I see! Be careful, Georgie. You could be doing yourself a disservice.'

'I've no idea what you're talking about. I've merely attempted to make myself look presentable, as a courtesy to my hostess.'

'Let's hope Reita appreciates your efforts in the spirit they're meant!'

At his irony, Georgie fired up.

'You seem to enjoy talking in riddles. Don't you think the female mind is capable of appreciating plain speaking? If you're trying to warn me against Mrs de Vries, why not come right out and say it? All I know against her is that she fancies your precious leopard as part of a coat. She's not the only woman in the world who likes furs, you know.'

Somehow, somewhere, she had ventured on to very dangerous ground. In the bungalow's narrow corridor they were not divided by very many steps, and now Niklaas took those steps, his hand snatching one of Georgies's slim wrists.

'No! You're so very right. Thank you for reminding me. What about you, Georgie? Are you one of those women who put their appearance before an animal's life?'

She tried to pull away, unavailingly.

'No, damn you, I'm not. By now you shouldn't need to ask how I feel about animals. Let go of my wrist—you're hurting me!' He *was* hurting her, but, strangely, he wasn't frightening her. Instead she was aware of a kind of suffocating excitement.

His grip slackened, but he did not release her. He

was close, very close in the confined area. She was vibrantly aware of him, his warmth, the subtle tang of the masculine odour she had come to associate with him. She was aware of his vivid green eyes roaming her face, her body.

'I'm not sure I know anything about you,' he said obscurely. 'But I do know I ought not to let you go to that damned house alone.'

'I won't be going alone. Dirk's collecting me . . .'

'That's not what I mean.' He paused as if assembling his thoughts, then, abruptly, 'Georgie, be careful of Dirk de Vries, but be especially careful of his mother. Don't believe everything they tell you, and don't . . .' He stopped, teeth catching at his lower lip.

'And don't what?' she queried, head tilted slightly to one side, unknowingly provocative, and immediately he released her.

'Oh, to hell with it. What am I worrying for? Why should I worry? You're old enough and probably experienced enough to take care of yourself.' He turned on his heel and disappeared into his own room, slamming the door.

CHAPTER FIVE

MARULA LODGE was a long low rambling stone-built house, set against the backdrop of an acacia plantation. The wide front was spanned by a veranda which, in its turn, commanded a view over the slope up which they had driven. This slope was overhung with masses of great trees, leaves gleaming now red, now gold in the fast-setting sun.

'What a beautiful home you have!' Georgie exclaimed. 'Aren't you lucky to live somewhere like this and in such a glorious setting?'

'You think so?' Dirk looked curiously at her rapt face. 'Let's stand here just for a moment, then,' he suggested. 'It'll be dark in a moment, and there's something I'd like you to see, something I think you'd appreciate.'

Then Georgie witnessed an incredible sight as the sun dropped out of view behind the trees, colour drained from the sky, leaving it pale, a pallor that became tinged first with a light clear green and then with flame, which almost at once was translated into a deep vibrant purple against which stars were suddenly visible. So, in the space of seconds, African day turned into night.

Georgie wondered if Niklaas ever watched the sun go down, or was that too impossibly romantic for him? Even so, she found herself wishing that this moment had been shared with him, instead of with Dirk.

'Quite something, isn't it?' Dirk had been

watching her expressive face, silhouetted as it was against one of the lamps that hung about the veranda.

'It was—oh, inexpressibly lovely. Thank you for showing it to me.' Turning impulsively towards him, she saw the obvious admiration in his face, and immediately her veil of reserve dropped back into place.

'Dirk, Dirk? Is that you out there? Whatever are you doing, keeping the young woman out on the veranda?' The imperious summons issued from within the sliding glass doors behind them.

'My mother,' Dirk said wryly.

The doors gave upon a spacious room, at least four times the size of the largest room at Niklaas's bungalow. The furnishings were of local wood, simple, but excellent in design, yet the room lacked warmth of character. After one swift glance, however, Georgie had eyes only for the woman who had bade them enter. It was obvious from which parent Dirk had inherited his thick marmalade thatch, though perhaps Reita de Vries's natural colouring was aided these days by artifice. Tall, dominating, as much by her bulk as by her height, she seemed to eclipse even the generous proportions of the room, to overwhelm the two who entered.

Dominating, Reita was also domineering, for it was she who dictated and directed the theme of their conversation as they ate. Georgie found herself resenting the impertinent inquisitiveness of the older woman.

'I must say I was surprised and—yes, displeased, to find that my son had employed a female assistant,' observed Mrs de Vries.

'Don't you believe in equal opportunities for

women?' Georgie asked. She had taken an instinctive dislike to the woman, and it took a heroic effort to keep her tone politely curious.

'Not in this kind of situation. Marula is a man's world, Miss Jonson, and best left to men.'

'Yet you live here?' Georgie pointed out.

An expression of annoyance distorted Reita de Vries's face, her already high colouring increasing.

'From necessity. My late husband's father was a fool. He tied up all the family wealth in an entail on this place, so that it can never be sold. Otherwise Dirk and I could be living a civilised existence now, in Johannesburg or at the Cape.'

'Well, I like Marula,' said Georgie. 'I wouldn't mind spending the rest of my life here.' She noticed Dirk's quick, interested glance, and cursed her defiant tongue. She didn't want him thinking she was after him, and through him Marula.

'But then, by all accounts, you are a very unfeminine young woman. You insist, I understand, on Niklaas treating you as an equal, upon sharing his accommodation.'

Georgie felt herself colouring, not with embarrassment, not just with annoyance at Reita's insufferable manner, but also at this total misrepresentation of her situation.

'I most certainly did not insist,' she began, but Reita de Vries was only interested in her own opinions.

'Dear Lysette, Niklaas's wife, was a delightfully feminine girl. She felt just as I do about Marula, but that impossible man insisted on immuring her here. He actually *expected* her to share his obsession with the place.'

'She must have known what Niklaas's life was

before she married him.' Georgie's anger was rising, and it was difficult to keep its resonance out of her voice. Even so, Reita looked at her sharply before replying.

'Naturally, but she did *not* expect to find him so totally wedded to his work that all her interests, particularly her social life, must be sacrificed. Dirk inherited Marula, but he doesn't find it necessary to devote every second of his life to it.'

'Perhaps,' Georgie said tautly, 'that's because he's the owner, not an employee. Niklaas works hard. He hasn't time to go gadding about even if he wanted to.'

Reita de Vries's bulk seemed to double itself as she subjected Georgie to a piercing scrutiny.

'Niklaas seems to have an unusually ardent champion in you, Miss Jonson. You would be a very foolish young woman if you entertained any "ideas" about him. I would be failing in my duty if I didn't warn you.'

'Mrs de Vries!' Georgie stood up and pushed back her chair. 'I'm a guest in your house, so I won't be rude, but I must tell you that I find your insinuations distasteful, and frankly I prefer to form my own judgements about people, including my colleague, Mr van der Walt. If you'll excuse me, I'd like to leave now. Dirk,' she turned to the man, who had remained silent throughout most of the meal, 'perhaps you'd lend me your Land Rover . . .?'

'Nonsense,' he rose, avoiding his mother's eye, 'I'll take you back to the bungalow myself. But must you leave? My mother was only . . .'

'I don't require you to make excuses for me, Dirk,' Reita de Vries interrupted. 'If the young woman wants to go, by all means let her. Any

romantic notions she entertains about Niklaas van
der Walt will very soon be disillusioned, as were
poor dear Lysette's.'

'I'm sorry you and Mother didn't hit it off,' Dirk
said, as they drove away from the Lodge. 'I had
hoped . . .' He shrugged. 'But there, the only woman
she ever approved of was Lysette.' His tone took on
a note of wry amusement. 'But she was already
married to Niklaas.'

Georgie didn't want to talk about Niklaas's wife.
Reita's decrying of his character had activated
Georgie's always strong sense of loyalty, making
her realise just how much she had come to like
Niklaas, even in so short a time, and whatever his
domestic problems had been she didn't want to hear
them from Reita's lips. As the Land Rover pulled
up at the perimeter of Niklaas's bungalow, she
asked:

'Dirk, why did you employ me, when you knew
Niklaas wouldn't want a female assistant?'

'I suppose I was considering my own tastes,
rather than his. I liked you, Georgie. I hoped,' his
words came hesitantly, 'that if you came out here to
work for me and we saw a lot of each other . . .'

'Dirk,' she interrupted, 'I . . .'

'Oh, I know it's early days. If you hadn't asked I
wouldn't have said anything yet, and I promise not
to make a nuisance of myself. But you will see me
again?'

'Yes, but . . .' Georgie also liked Dirk. She had
known he would be an easy man to work for, but she
knew quite as certainly that the liking would never
go any further.

'When will you come out with me again? We

needn't go up to the Lodge next time,' he added hastily.

'I don't know. It depends on our work schedule.' She felt for the door handle of the jeep, suddenly afraid that he might expect to kiss her.

'You *are* entitled to time off,' he reminded her, 'and I am your boss.'

'I know, but . . .'

'OK, Georgie, we'll play it your way.' He reached across and located the door handle, for which she still fumbled, and brushed his lips across her cheek. The sensation moved her not at all. She felt no pleasure, no revulsion. It might have been a brother's kiss.

'Goodnight, Georgie, and don't be too hard on Mother. She only said what she did for your own good. *I* don't like the idea of your being here alone with Nik. I wish I'd been home when you arrived. I'd intended you to lodge with one of the wardens and his wife. Are you sure you wouldn't like me to . . .?'

'Quite sure.' Thankful that the door was now open, Georgie slipped down from the high seat.

'Perhaps your mother did mean well,' she said, though without conviction, her clear voice carrying further on the night air than she knew. 'But it was quite unnecessary. I'm not afraid of Niklaas.'

Since no lights showed in the bungalow, Georgie was a little anxious that she might find herself locked out. She need not have worried. Apparently there was no need for locks and bolts out here in the middle of the reserve. The door opened easily.

She removed her shoes and began to tiptoe along the passageway. Niklaas, she felt sure, would not appreciate being disturbed by her late return. She hadn't intentionally defied him, but the drive back and the ensuing conversation with Dirk had taken longer than she'd realised.

She actually had her hand on the latch of her door, when all the corridor lights came on and she swung round to face Niklaas. He was, she noticed, an uneasy pulse leaping in her throat, wearing only a thigh-length robe that left a disturbing view of long bronzed muscular legs. Apparently he disdained such conventional garments as pyjamas.

'I thought perhaps you'd decided to stay the night,' he said, his voice harsh.

'If I'd been invited, I might have done.' Georgie knew she would have refused most emphatically to pass a night under Reita de Vries's roof. Her reply was a statement of her liberty to do as she chose, but it seemed to annoy him disproportionately.

He moved closer, and she could see the expanse of muscular chest left bare by the opening of his robe, a vee of chest plentifully covered in hair only a little lighter than that of the burnished head looming over her, as she stared up at him, feeling disadvantaged by the removal of her high-heeled shoes.

'You wouldn't have received an invitation from Reita,' he said with a conviction which Georgie knew was not misplaced. 'Though Dirk might have obliged, if his mother had been away from home. Do you know what time it is?' he demanded before she could tell him what she thought of his insinuation.

'I've no idea. I forgot to wear my watch, and time passes very quickly when you're enjoying yourself.' She had no intention of letting Niklaas know that as a social occasion the evening had been a failure. The most enjoyable part had been witnessing the sunset and, she admitted, the drive back, knowing that she was returning to the protection of Niklaas's roof. Reita's denigration of him had put her own feelings into perspective.

'You enjoyed yourself at the lodge?' Niklaas was coldly comtemptuous. 'So you're one of their kind?' He turned on his heel to go back into his room, but an incensed Georgie moved swiftly between him and the door. There was no time to marvel at her own daring, and while she might have defended him to Reita de Vries she had not deluded herself into thinking that, for the future, their relationship was going to be a smooth one.

'I'm just about fed up with your innuendoes and your obscure exit lines!' she told him, her blue eyes darkening to stormy violet. 'Just what sort are the de Vrieses? What sort do you think *I* am?'

'The de Vrieses, as if you hadn't already discovered it for yourself, are extremely rich, rich enough to tempt any young woman with a mercenary streak. Klaus de Vries admitted to me once that he'd made a bad mistake when he married Reita. She was just a little shopgirl from Jo'burg, and all she saw in Marula was money—not its beauty, but the money she needed to support the life-style she craved. Fortunately, her father-in-law saw through her even before Klaus did, before she could do any harm.'

'Well, I'm not . . .' Georgie began, but he swept on.

'. . . and Dirk's very much her son. He goes after what he wants, regardless of the cost to others. Do you think I didn't notice the way he was looking at

you this afternoon? It's obvious why he picked you
for this job. You won't have to work very hard to
catch him, if you can manage to ingratiate yourself
with Reita.'

'Well, that shouldn't trouble you, should it?' she
retorted. 'And as it happens you're right. I am
aware that Dirk likes me.' She had the satisfaction
of seeing his jaw clench. 'But what makes you think
I want to catch him?'

'The way you jumped at his invitation. The way
you sat outside with him in his car just now, for over
an hour.'

'You were spying on me?' Georgie was outraged.
The fact that she'd been doing nothing of which she
need be ashamed was beside the point. How dared
he pry into her affairs? He had no right, no interest.

'I was looking out for your return, not spying. I
happened to be at the window when I saw the Land
Rover's lights. I can also,' sarcastically, 'tell the
time, so I know exactly how long it was between
your arrival and Dirk's departure.'

'We were just talking.' She felt like a reprimand-
ed teenager facing an irate father, and she didn't
have to defend her behaviour to Niklaas, she
thought furiously, or try to justify herself. All the
same, she didn't like to think of him imagining . . .

'Just talking!' he snorted. 'I know Dirk de Vries,
and if you're telling me he could spend an hour
cooped up with a girl looking as you do now,
without . . . without . . .' He swallowed suddenly
and took a step backwards.

Georgie was beyond thinking of consequences.

'Just how do I look, Niklaas?' she enquired with
dangerous quietness, deliberately taking a step
closer to him. Her fingers itched to slap him, and if

he insulted her in the way she thought he was implying . . .

'You look,' he said thickly, 'like a woman who's got herself up purposely to allure, tempting bait for any red-blooded man.'

'Like Dirk?' she said with icy sweetness. 'I mean, it wouldn't worry *you*, of course, since you haven't a red corpuscle in your entire bloodstream.'

Niklaas made a sound pitched somewhere between a growl and a groan, and then the square-cut edges of his fingernails were digging into her bare shoulders, she was trapped between him and the wall.

'Don't be too sure of that.' The vibrancy of his voice was no longer attributable to anger. 'Just because I choose to avoid women it doesn't mean I don't have the normal urges.'

For the first time a little stab of remembered fear touched Georgie, as she felt the increasing muscular hardness of his body against hers. She'd meant to taunt, to annoy, to provoke, but not into this kind of response.

'I think I'd better go,' she whispered. 'It's late and . . .'

He chose to misinterpret her meaning.

'You're right—it is late, far too late to draw back now. You want to know if I'm as much of a man as de Vries? I'll show you!'

A large hand moved beneath her chin, to force her face up to his, and Georgie gasped, not with pain, not with fear, though that too was present, but only as a small distant voice from the past. She gasped at a sensation she had never thought to experience, a pang of desire.

Niklaas's mouth closed over hers. He was being

deliberately rough, then momentary surprise made him check for a moment as she made no attempt to bar her mouth to him, as he found that his tongue had no need to force its relentless, exploring passage. Hands against his shoulders, her fingers bit into the hard muscles, clawed their way upwards until they were clenched in the unruly auburn hair.

Subtly his mood changed. It was no longer aggressive, his lips had softened, the invasion of his tongue was now sincerely urgent. He slid the thin straps of her dress from her shoulders, his mouth moving to kiss her neck. Trembling, she clung to him, as his mouth discovered her ear, playing with it, then trailed a fiery course back to her mouth. He kissed all round her lips, delicately grazing on the soft lower lip, tracing its outline with his tongue. His hands had shaped their way down to her hips, their movements druggingly caressive.

All that seemed to matter was that he should continue to kiss her, kiss and hold her. She was totally relaxed against him, her lips parted, her breathing unsteady. But he held her away from him.

'Not so fast,' he whispered, his deep voice rough and uneven. 'First tell me, Georgie, do I have red blood in my veins or not?'

'Yes, Niklaas, oh yes!' she whispered.

He took her mouth again then, with deep, searching kisses. Her arms around his waist, she pressed against him. Her dress had slipped completely from her shoulders and Niklaas had possessed himself of one breast, his fingers lightly tantalising its central peak into pulsating life. As his mouth followed the erection his hands had created, she cradled his head, running her hands through the sensuous thickness of his hair.

'Georgie!' Slowly he was drawing her with him, towards the open door of his bedroom. 'Georgie, I want you—now!'

If he hadn't spoken, she told herself afterwards, she might have gone with him unresistingly. It was his words that reminded her, words that she had heard spoken before, roughly, lustfully, by a man who had refused to take her 'no' for an answer.

She went rigid in his arms, felt the sudden bile rise in her throat. Then she was wrenching herself free, running for the bathroom, with barely enough time to lock the door before the contents of her stomach erupted in great heaving retches mingled with a violent sobbing that seemed as if it would tear her apart. Above the noise of her own wretchedness she could hear Niklaas hammering on the door, demanding entrance.

At last the terrible spasms ceased, and leaning weakly against the basin, she splashed cold water on her face, rinsed her mouth.

'Georgie!, Georgie—let me in! What the hell——'

'Go *away*, Niklaas,' she begged weakly. 'Just go away and leave me alone.'

There was silence, then:

'I'll leave you alone all right. I won't come near you!' His voice was harsh. 'But just come out of there.'

'If I do you won't . . .'

'My God, do you think I'd touch you now? What do you take me for?'

Of course, some men were revolted by physical illness. He probably thought she had been drinking at the de Vrieses. Well, that was better than that he should know the truth about her sudden revulsion.

With trembling hands she unlocked the door and emerged, head down. Humiliation flooded her. She felt shrunken, diminished, vulnerable.

'Go to bed, Georgie.' It was said wearily.

She nodded without speaking. It seemed a million miles to her door, and once inside she leant there, hearing his slam violently. Limply she undressed, her clothes spilling into a silken pool where she had stepped out of them. She crawled beneath the bedclothes, shivering, not with cold, but with a terrible aching, unassuaged longing.

Right from the first she had experienced, without recognising it, the nature of Niklaas's effect on her. Tonight she had been forced to realise what it was. It was something no other man had ever caused her to feel, a response she could have sworn no man would ever extract from her. She should have guessed earlier that evening when she had been driven to defend him against Reita's slurs, but it had taken those moments in his arms to open her eyes to her own foolishness, her heart's perfidy. She had done the one thing she should not have done. She had fallen in love, and at the moment of recognition the past had loomed up to remind her of its one remaining shadow, that she was not fit for any man, but especially this one, to love. She had been irrevocably, unspeakably defiled.

She tossed and turned on her bed, unavailingly seeking oblivion in sleep, release from the terrible hungry anguish her body felt. And how would she face Niklaas in the morning? She would feel embarrassment. And Niklaas? He would be back to his old, cold, unapproachable self once more, hating her for being the cause of a weakness he despised.

Not surprisingly, when she did finally fall asleep,

she overslept, and at first she could not identify the
source of the loud hammering that pounded in her
head. Then she realised that someone was knocking
at her door.

'Georgie, for God's sake, wake up, quickly! I
need you!'

For a moment her heart leapt erratically, but then
she realised Niklaas's tone was that of the professional vet, not the lover, and she scrabbled hastily
into her clothes, wondering what disaster merited
such urgency, but thankful for its existence, which
would help to smooth over their next encounter.

'It's an emergency,' he told her briefly as she
emerged from the bungalow. 'I'll explain as we go.'

They were heading for the surgery—some animal
must have been badly hurt. But this conjecture on
her part was soon dispelled.

'I don't suppose you've ever seen a badly injured
man? It's somewhat different from tending a sick
animal. I wouldn't have called you out if I could
have managed alone.'

'A man?' Georgie queried.

'Yes!' He was out of the jeep and striding towards
the buildings, so that she had to run to keep up with
him.

A group of African villagers milled about outside,
their birdlike chatter shrill, alarmed, and Niklaas
spoke a few brief words over his shoulder as he
pushed open the surgery door. Immediately a hush
fell and they began to disperse. Now Georgie saw
the reason for their hysterical concern. It was
Mugongo, their chief, who lay upon the table,
ominously still, the yellowish pigment of his face
tinged with grey. The whole of his upper right arm
seemed to be a mass of torn and bleeding flesh.

Niklaas swore expressively and went into action.

'Thank God it didn't get the artery, or we might have been too late.'

He was as much doctor as vet, Georgie marvelled, as she passed swabs and instruments, watched the deft movements of his fingers as he made order of what seemed to her to be a ghastly mess. To her amazement he used no anaesthetic on the wounded man, nor did Mugongo make any outcry, lying there in stolid silence. Only when the injury was finally stitched and dressed did she venture to question Niklaas.

'Africans are brave about physical pain if the injury is a visible one. It's invisible things like headache or stomach-ache that get them down. All their old superstitions well up and they think they've been bewitched. Mugongo knows this was his own damned stupid fault. Thanks, Georgie,' he added, 'I couldn't have managed without you.'

She was sure he could, but she glowed nevertheless.

'I didn't know you could cope with human injuries!' She covered her pleasure with a laugh. 'I shall feel a whole lot safer myself in future.'

'Will you?' There was double meaning in his words and his glance, and Georgie flushed. In her absorption with their task, the events of last night had been mercifully blanked out. Now her embarrassment returned in full force, but he was answering her, ignoring the confusion he'd wrought.

'Out here, a medicine man, as the natives call us, has to be all things to all people as well as to animals. At times of dire need humans have no objection to being treated by a vet.'

Two game guards carried Mugongo away to his own hut where, Niklaas said, he would be well cared for by his womenfolk.

'You said Mugongo's injury was his own fault? What happened?' asked Georgie as they cleaned up the surgery.

'The bloody fool went into the leopard's pen. He thought it was sick, and instead of waiting for me . . .'

'The leopard attacked him?'

'Yes. I told you they were unpredictable creatures, and that,' savagely, 'means that after all the work we put in on him, he'll have to be destroyed.'

'Oh no! Why?'

'Because an animal that's once tasted human blood will attack again. I can't release a creature like that into the wild.' As Niklaas spoke he reached for his gun, ramming home the syringe which Georgie knew held a lethal shot. She caught his arm, looked up at him, her face pale, eyes pleading.

'Isn't there any other way? Couldn't he be sent to a zoo or something?'

'At Dirk's expense? Besides, you know what I think of zoos!'

'Perhaps if I asked him?' she began.

'Don't flatter yourself! Whatever influence you may have with Dirk would be outweighed by his mother. And that's another thing. I don't want the de Vrieses to know what's happened here this morning. As far as they're concerned, the animal recovered and was released. That damned woman's not getting its skin.'

'But how will you . . .?'

'My men will dispose of the body safely.'

'Can you trust them not to speak of it?'

Niklaas gave a grunt of a laugh.

'No danger. Dirk doesn't understand their lingo. He's never troubled himself with things like that.'

'But you did?' Georgie followed him towards the leopard's enclosure.

'When Dirk and I were kids, he was always ailing, shut up in a stuffy nursery, or being dragged to this or that hospital. Oom Klaus took me everywhere with him. He spoke several dialects, and I picked them up. It's been a useful accomplishment.' He stopped, and Georgie heard the click as he cocked the rifle. She drew in a little breath and he looked sideways at her. 'You don't have to watch, you know.'

'You mean I should walk away?' she retorted.

'Suit yourself.'

After that, all Georgie could do was to stand and watch as Niklaas waited patiently for the restless leopard to present the best target. The beautiful animal had been recovering so well from the operation on its eye, an operation in which she had a personal stake. Another few days, and they would have been able to return it to its natural habitat. Despite herself, Georgie felt her eyes sting and her lips tremble, but she forced herself to remain.

The shot rang out. Niklaas's aim was sure, and almost immediately the drug took effect. As the animal slumped to the ground, the sunlight highlighting its beautiful pelt, Georgie felt her throat convulse and she turned away, saying, while she could still speak:

'Well, that's that, then. What now?'

She climbed into the jeep and sat in frozen silence, fighting her emotions. Niklaas, she saw, had entered the pen, followed by two of the

Africans, and was inspecting the body. Seconds later they all emerged, the Africans carrying the leopard. Niklaas must have issued his instructions for its disposal. As he strode towards his side of the jeep, Georgie stared out of her window, feigning indifference, but her tightly interlaced fingers, their knuckles white, betrayed her.

Niklaas said nothing, but his arm went round her shoulders, pulling her towards him, so that her head rested against his chest, destroying all her carefully erected defences. She gulped once, then the tears came. His grasp tightened, and she felt his chest lurch unsteadily just once, before his breathing returned to its normal, regular rythmn. At last she pulled away, and he handed her his handkerchief.

'I'm sorry,' she choked.

'If it will make you feel any better,' he said, his voice oddly taut, 'Mugongo was right. The animal was sick—the infection had begun to spread to the other eye. It would have had to be destroyed anyway.'

Georgie nodded dumbly. It did help, but she was not yet quite mistress of her emotions. She had an urgent need to feel his arms round her again. But his embrace this morning had been an impersonal one, a soothing gesture he might have made to a child. It was as if he'd read her mind.

'And, Georgie,' he spoke hesitantly, 'I'm sorry about last night.'

'So am I. I didn't mean to . . . it's just that I c-can't . . .' If only she could explain, but she could never tell Niklaas about Ralph. She was afraid of the revulsion she would see in his eyes. 'It was . . . it was . . .' Since she couldn't tell him the truth about what it had been to her, she faltered into silence, but he put his own interpretation on her words.

'You're right. It was a mistake, plus crass
stupidity and arrogance on my part. But you caught
me on the raw, particularly where de Vries is
concerned. But you couldn't know what he...'
Hurriedly he changed tack. 'Well, it won't happen
again, ever. You have my assurance.'

She could only stare at him, the tears spilling over
once again. She wanted it to happen again, wanted
to be held by him, kissed by him. But even if he had
wanted the same thing, she must not let him.

'I mean it, Georgie. Don't you believe me? It
mustn't happen again, or your job here is finished.'

Indignation stemmed the flood of her tears.

'I wasn't the only one involved, you know!'

'Exactly, and I was blaming myself. I don't want
involvement, Georgie, emotional scenes. We're
colleagues, and that's the way it has to stay. That's
what you want, isn't it?'

'Yes, yes, of course,' she agreed hastily. But she
had to ask: 'But, Niklaas, I can't believe you don't
have *some* feelings. You may not want involvement,
but suppose, some day, somebody else does?'

'Somebody else?' suspiciously. 'You're not referring to yourself?'

'No,' she lied. 'It was just a theoretical question.
Niklaas, why do you pretend you're cold? How can
you let one woman ruin the rest of your life? You
weren't meant to be a monk. It isn't healthy to deny
natural needs. Everyone needs love.'

'Shut up, damn you! I . . .'

'Were you still in love with your wife, when she
left you?'

'That's none of your damned business!'

'No, maybe, but I can draw my own conclusions.'

'You're a blasted nuisance, do you know that, Georgie? I don't want to be reminded of that time, of what I felt. I've put it behind me, or I had until you came here. Of course I'm still capable of feeling, of physical feeling, but that's not what we're talking about, is it? Like all women, what you want to do is to pry into my "emotions". All right—, yes, I was still in love with Lysette when she left me. We hadn't been married that long, and at first I thought everything was going to be wonderful, happy ever after,' he jeered. 'Well, it was wonderful at first, especially the sex. Lysette was a very sexy lady.'

'Oh!' Georgie whispered, misery twisting her in its painful grip.

'My biggest mistake was that I didn't find out enough about her before I married her. I was infatuated, perhaps I should say "fatuous".'

'And she must have loved you?'

'Yes, or at least she wanted me. It isn't necessarily the same thing, you know.'

'I know,' she whispered. Niklaas had wanted her, but he didn't love her. Thank God he didn't know just how unlovable she really was.

'Are you a virgin, Georgie?'

Oh God, was he a mind-reader?

'Why?' Immediately she was on the defensive.

'I have a good reason for asking.' His tone was gentle.

'I . . . I . . .' She couldn't lie to Niklaas of all people, but the words wouldn't come.

'Of course you are,' he said impatiently. 'I shouldn't have had to ask. So don't get any noble ideas about feeling sorry for me, Georgie, offering me your body. I don't take virgins. A first relationship is too important to a woman. Once they've experienced sex, the man assumes a greater importance in their eyes, their emotions become involved. They can't treat it as men do, a satisfaction of physical need, a satisfaction they can obtain from someone completely different the next time around. When you first make love, Georgie,' his voice softened, 'it's got to be with someone who feels as you do, who wants to share everything with you, not just sex, but emotional and physical involvement too. You're that kind of girl.'

'But I wasn't . . .'

'No buts, Georgie. I'm not for you. Understand that once and for all. For my needs I turn to sophisticated women, women who feel the way I do, no complications. That's not for you.'

'You're right, of course,' she began.

'I know, so let's get off the damned subject, shall we? What you need right now is a cup of coffee. It's been a very emotional morning for you. You're not thinking straight.'

CHAPTER SIX

As the weeks passed, Georgie knew exquisite torture, working side by side with Niklaas. He no longer seemed to resent her presence, but his manner towards her was consistently businesslike. He treated her exactly as he would any colleague. That was what she'd wanted originally, but oh, not now.

Only in the privacy of her bedroom dared she admit to herself just how deeply her emotions were involved, and this left a biting frustration that could only be quelled by work and still more work, while in her spare time, as a panacea against idleness, she accepted the invitations Dirk still regularly issued.

Niklaas too worked like a man possessed, and Georgie could not help wondering if, in spite of his iron self-control, he found it difficult to banish the remembrance of what had passed between them, what had so nearly been. Many a time, even though her head was lowered over some task, she was aware that his eyes rested thoughtfully upon her. But she made certain at such times that she never met that gaze. For the sake of her own peace of mind, the only rational course was to keep him at arm's length, literally, making sure that not even their fingers brushed in accidental contact. She didn't think she could take another emotional confrontation with Niklaas without revealing her need of him.

She lay awake far into the night, every night,

trying to decide on her best course of action. Should she leave Marula, hoping that distance would break the spell of a hopeless enchantment?

Since taking up her post at Marula, Georgie had received one or two letters from Hendrik Beit, the young scientist she had met at the Kruger National Park, but she had been kept so busy that she had only answered the first letter, and since then, apart from the occasions when his letters arrived, she had almost forgotten his existence. So his unexpected arrival, expressly to see her, though flattering, was not precisely what she would have wished. Niklaas too seemed to disapprove.

'Just because young Beit's on holiday, I hope you won't be expecting time off. It's not as if you know him very well.'

'Have I *asked* for time off?' she retorted, and indeed the idea had never even occurred to her. She was quite content to go on working without a break, if it would keep her at Niklaas's side. For that had been her decision, even though there were moments of tension, when he made it obvious that he too was avoiding any physical contact with her.

'No, you haven't asked, but I'm letting you know, before you *do* ask, that it won't be granted. If young Beit wants to moon around after you, it'll have to be in your free time, when you're not out with de Vries instead.'

Though Georgie had been out several times with Dirk, it had not been beyond the bounds of Marula, nor had she asked for Hendrik's attentions, and Niklaas's attitude made her see red.

'Thank you so much!' she said sarcastically. 'Well, in that case, don't expect me to work overtime, as I often do. Just because you don't have a social life, don't expect me to become a recluse.'

Oddly, Dirk de Vries, despite his reiterated interest in her, had made no demur about her visitor, and Hendrik was actually staying at Marula Lodge. Dirk had even suggested that she might like some time off, but she had politely refused. She didn't want Niklaas to think she'd been behind his back to their employer, nor did she intend to give Hendrick the idea that his company was that important to her. It wouldn't be fair to the young man.

However, apart from evenings, she was permitted one full day, Sunday, and, after a week of conversing under Niklaas's jaundiced eye, Hendrik asked if they couldn't contrive to get away from the bungalow.

'De Vries has offered me the use of a Land Rover tomorrow. Even though we can't get off Marula in the time, we could get away from van der Walt. Funny,' he added, sounding a little hurt, 'we always used to get on well when I worked here. Now he glowers at me as if I were his worst enemy. If I didn't know old Nik so well, I'd say he was jealous.'

'It's certainly nothing like that. He's only just come to accept my presence here, to admit that I'm a good vet. He's a confirmed woman-hater.'

'Everyone knows that,' Hendrik agreed. 'They know why, too, and about the dance his wife led him. Which is why his dog-in-the-manger attitude puzzles me. But let's forget him, for heaven's sake, and enjoy ourselves, hmm?'

They set out early, to make the most of the day. A grim-faced Niklaas observed their preparations for departure.

'Be back before dusk, Beit! Tomorrow is a

working day for us. When,' he added, with heavy emphasis, 'is your holiday up?'

'Tuesday, unfortunately,' Hendrik grimaced, 'but I'm due some more time next month, so I'll be back.'

Georgie thought Niklaas looked less than enchanted by the prospect.

'He's changed somehow,' Hendrik reiterated, as they drove away from the bungalow, Georgie uncomfortably aware of Niklaas on the veranda, the green glitter of his gaze seeming to pierce the flesh between her shoulder-blades, even through the tarpaulin cover of the Land Rover.

The sun baked down from an almost colourless sky, sucking every scrap of moisture it could out of the ground and the vegetation.

'The rainy season's late this year,' commented Hendrik, as their passage threw up clouds of fine, powdery soil, coating their vehicle's bonnet and even permeating the interior through gaps in windows and canvas top. 'It usually starts in late November, but here we are, well into December, and not a sign of a break in the weather. When it does break, it'll be with a vengeance.'

Hendrik was an interesting companion, an intellectual, but above all very much the scientist. He was particularly anxious to catch a sight of some white rhinoceros which Niklaas had persuaded Dirk to have imported into Marula, an important exercise in conservation, since they were an endangered species.

'When I say white,' Hendrik laughed a little, 'don't go expecting some pure, beautiful, mystical creature like a unicorn. To the uninitiated they look much like any other rhino. For white, read a rather dirty grey. The main difference is in their physical appearance and their placid temperament.'

They didn't see the white rhino.

'I wish now I'd asked Niklaas where to find them, but he wasn't very approachable, was he?'

They moved on, and Hendrik began to point out familiar landmarks which he recalled from his term of employment at Marula.

'In some ways I'm sorry I left. There's more scope for scientific experiment at the Kruger, of course, but it *is* so much bigger and more impersonal. And,' he added, 'I wouldn't mind being back here now, so I could see more of you.'

Georgie didn't know whether to turn aside his remark with a laugh or whether to make it clear he was wasting his time so far as she was concerned. She decided on the laugh. His words could have been purely flirtatious.

It was late afternoon when they came to the waterhole, where a hide was provided for tourist parties. Since it was out of season they would, Hendrik pointed out, have the facility to themselves. Looking at her watch, however, Georgie protested that perhaps they should be starting on their return journey and asked him if he'd forgotten Niklaas's injunction that they should be back before dusk.

'I haven't forgotten, and we will be. We've made a circular tour. Remember, I know this territory, and we're two-thirds of the way back already.' He already knew that there hadn't been time in her busy schedule to observe the comings and goings at a well-used waterhole. 'It's an experience not to be missed.'

Georgie allowed herself to be persuaded.

'But only for half an hour,' she warned.

It was as rewarding as Hendrik had promised. A waterbuck was their first sighting, stepping daintily on fragile legs down a hippo path that led to the water's edge. Then came wildebeest and their inevitable zebra companions, timorous and hesitant, their Arab-like heads lifted in caution before they drank. A snake swam swiftly across the pool, and ostriches made a parade of their arrival, strutting through the reedy edges of the waterhole. Entranced, Georgie forgot the passage of time, until a glance towards Hendrik made her realise she could no longer make out the individual features of his absorbed profile.

'It's late—we must go. Niklaas will be furious!'

'He's only your boss in working hours,' Hendrik pointed out.

'Yes, but in those hours he expects me to be efficient and wide awake, and if we're too late getting back I won't be.'

Because of speed restrictions imposed for the safety of the wild life, they couldn't drive as fast as Georgie would have liked. Then the rain began, quite suddenly, with no prior warning other than a fitful wind. It was a drenching rain that quickly churned the dust into a quagmire, and Georgie remembered with a sudden stab of alarm that they had not yet recrossed the river that ran through Marula.

A flash of lightning illuminated the horizon. Thunder rolled and muttered. The wind gusted more strongly. As the elements became more violent they reached the river, and to Georgie's relief forded the now faster moving water without incident. But conditions for driving were worsening. The rain was pelting down in solid, blinding sheets, and the windscreen wipers were unable to cope with their task.

'We'll have to stop and wait out the storm,' Hendrik decided.

'Oh, but . . .'

'It would be foolhardy to go on, Georgie. Even van der Walt would have to agree. We can't see a hand's breadth in front of us. We could drive straight into a tree, or this damned storm might bring one down in front of us.'

And, indeed, already giant hands were wrenching at branches, the air alive with whirling debris of every conceivable kind. Hendrick ran the vehicle into the shelter of a clump of low-growing trees, whose drooping, heavy branches formed a protective canopy over them.

'Now what?' asked Georgie. She wasn't frightened of the storm, even though it outdid by fifty per cent the intensity of any she had ever experienced.

'We stay put. There's no telling how long this'll go on. In fact, I suggest we stretch out in the back and get some shut-eye. Then, when it clears up, we'll be able to go on and you'll still be bright-eyed and bushy-tailed for Sir.'

This reminder of Niklaas made Georgie shiver. He was *not* going to be pleased.

Hours later, the storm still showed no signs of abating; and Georgie fell at last into a restless slumber. The storm had chilled the air, and without the engine there was no warmth in the vehicle's interior. At some time during the night, instinctively, she must have sought the nearest source of warmth, Hendrik's lean young body. For when she woke it was with a start, to two uncomfortable, embarrassing realisations. She was firmly clamped,

by one of his arms, to a still sleeping Hendrik, and
the sound that had disturbed her was Niklaas's
voice, raised in anger. The driver's door was open
and his eyes were glaring at what must appear to
him to be a very intimate scene. She struggled to
free herself, but in heavy slumber Hendrik protested inarticulately, tightening his grip.

'*Let go of her*!' roared Niklaas, and his bass fury
achieved what Georgie's efforts could not. Hendrik's arm fell away and he sat up, bleary-eyed,
groping ineffectually for the spectacles he had left
in the driver's cab.

'Georgie! Get out of there!'

They emerged simultaneously, Georgie with an
attempt at dignity, Hendrik unsteadily, glasses in
hand.

'Don't put them on!' Niklaas ordered, and as the
young scientist peered at him uncomprehendingly,
'I've never yet hit a man in spectacles.'

In an instant Georgie was at his side, both hands
grasping his right arm.

'Niklaas, no! You can't—you mustn't! There's no
earthly reason . . .'

But Niklaas, it seemed, was beyond reason. His
whole frame was shaking, and, his impetus taking
Georgie with him, her slight weight hampering him
not at all, he struck out. She had forgotten he was
left-handed.

Hendrik sprawled in the mud, looked up in
pained bewilderment, a hand held to his jaw.

'What the hell was that for? It's not my fault there
was a storm.'

'Maybe not!' Niklaas's retort was curt. 'But you
took full advantage of it, didn't you?' His meaning
dawned simultaneously on Hendrik and Georgie.

'*I say*!' the young man began, but Georgie's tongue was quicker.

'You foul-minded pig! Don't you dare! You judge everyone by your own standards. Just because *you* would have——' Her voice faltered, because she knew Niklaas would not have taken advantage of her any more than Hendrik had done.

She had released his arm, but now it was he who took her elbow, crushing it in a vicious grip, as he propelled her across the storm-rutted ground to where his jeep stood.

'You're coming with me,' he said grimly, and over his shoulder to the young man just scrambling to his feet, 'You can make your own way back. If you're wise you'll get out of Marula today!'

'You can't do that!' protested Georgie, as Niklaas's vehicle surged away. 'It's not up to you to cut short his holiday, to throw him out of the park. He's Dirk's guest.'

'And you're my assistant, and he's interfered with your work long enough.'

'Rubbish!' snapped Georgie. 'My work hasn't suffered at all this last week, and you know it. In fact, you've made sure I've worked a darn sight harder than usual. Hendrick was right about you,' she continued, heedless of the danger she was incurring. 'He said you were acting like a dog in the manger, and you were. You are. You don't want to get involved with me yourself, but you can't bear the thought that anyone else might. You're not human, Niklaas van der Walt. But you're not a dog, you're a cowardly jackal, that's encountered something he can't cope with. Yet he won't let it alone, but hangs and sniffs around, afraid someone else might carry it off.'

As Hendrik had said, they'd not been too far from
the bungalow when the storm began. If it had only
broken ten minutes later! The angry exchange of
words was scarcely over as Niklaas braked and
rounded the vehicle in four lithe, dangerous strides.
Her accusation that he was inhuman might almost
have been borne out by his angry snarl as he
snatched her from her seat and dragged her up the
steps and across the veranda, moving so swiftly that
she stumbled in his wake, several times very nearly
falling. In the living-room he flung her into a chair
and stood over her.

She noticed that he seemed to be shaking
uncontrollably, perspiration standing out on his
brow, and she wondered incredulously at this
apparent total loss of control in so rigidly unbending
a man.

'*You dare*! To compare *me* to an animal, when
your own behaviour resembles that of a bitch on
heat. First you're in my arms, making my life
intolerable, trying to destroy all my resolutions.
Then, when I manage to resist you, the lures you
threw out, you run around with de Vries, and to top
it all you spend a night with young Beit!'

'Hendrik and I did *not* spend the night together,
not in the way you mean. We slept in the back of the
Land Rover because it was the only sensible thing to
do. We'd have been here in plenty of time for office
hours. But you had to come poking your arrogant,
prying nose, and I believe you *wanted* to find what
you did, so that you could deliberately misinterpret
it.' Georgie choked back a sob. 'Well, I hope you're
satisfied.' Defiantly, she rose from the chair,
surprised when he made no attempt to restrain her,
and gained the comparative safety of her room.

Niklaas's accusations had driven her beyond tears. She was furiously angry, remained angry as she showered and put on fresh clothes. How on earth could she have believed for one moment that she loved this egotistical, hurtful man?

She had long since worked out her trial period, she realised, and there had been no suggestion of her incompetence. Very well! So there would be no ignominy in her leaving. She had given Marula a trial, had given Niklaas van der Walt a trial, and found him wanting. She'd see Dirk today and hand in her notice. Moreover, she would tell him exactly why she was leaving, and suggest, if he had any more freakish ideas about wishing a female assistant on to his chief veterinary, that he should dismiss the notion, for the woman's sake.

Keyed up to tell Niklaas of her decision, she was deflated to find him gone. Damn it! That left her without transport. How was she supposed to go to the surgery, let alone to Marula Lodge? It certainly wasn't possible, or safe, to go on foot.

The sound of an engine took her on to the veranda. He must have relented and come back for her. But no, it was Hendrik, looking dismally sorry for himself, clothes caked in mud, a swelling on his jaw. He came painfully up the steps.

'Van der Walt not about?' he asked with a trace of uneasiness. 'I thought I'd better check to see if you were OK.'

'He's not here,' she reassured him. 'The wretched man's taken himself off and left me stranded. Probably done it on purpose, so I can't get to work. Then he'll complain to Dirk, before I can complain about him.'

'No problem. I'll run you wherever you want to

go. And, Georgie, I think,' he added awkwardly,
'I'd best be on my way today. I don't particularly
fancy another run-in with Niklaas. He seems to
resent anyone else hanging around you. I didn't
realise you two . . .'

'There's nothing between Niklaas and me,'
Georgie sighed.

'But you wish there were?' the young man said
shrewdly.

If only it were as simple as that!

At the surgery there was no sign of Niklaas. The
whole place was securely locked up.

'May as well go on to the Lodge?' Hendrik
suggested.

'I do want to see Dirk, but Niklaas won't be
there,' said Georgie. 'I once heard him say he'd
never cross their threshold again. There seems to be
some bad feeling between him and Dirk.'

'That's putting it mildly,' the young scientist told
her. 'It has to do with Lysette, Niklaas's wife. After
a couple of months' marriage to van der Walt, she
started running around with de Vries. They were
always off to Jo'burg, or the Cape.'

Their arrival at he Lodge prevented the further
questions Georgie would have liked to ask, and it
was Dirk himself who strolled out to meet them.

'Georgie, is something wrong? Something you
can't handle?'

'The surgery's all locked up,' she explained, 'and
I've no idea where Niklaas is.' Forgetting her
intention to complain about Niklaas and hand in
her resignation, she was aware of growing anxiety.
Niklaas had left the bungalow in a strangely
disturbed state, and it wasn't like him to break

routine. First thing in the morning he always went immediately to his surgery.

'So you didn't meet him on your way down?'

'Should we have done?'

'Yes, I sent him home. He was in no fit condition to work.'

'*He's ill*?' Georgie exclaimed.

'I went out to the surgery to consult him about one of our dogs, and when I saw the state he was in I told him to leave everything to you for a day or two.'

'But what's wrong with him?' Anxiety had become alarm.

'Only an attack of malaria,' Dirk said unconcernedly. 'We all suffer with it from time to time, don't we, Beit?'

Of course! The trembling, the perspiration that she'd put down to strong emotion. She should have guessed. No wonder he'd been in such a vile mood, having to search for her when he felt so unwell.

'I'd better get back to the bungalow,' she decided.

'Nonsense.' Dirk shook his head. 'He'll cope, take the usual drugs and sleep it off. Your job is to see to the animals.'

'Look,' Hendrik broke in eagerly, 'I could stay on for a few more days, just until van der Walt's back on his feet. There's too much for one person to do here, especially for a woman.'

Georgie bristled immediately, but before she could explode in defence of her own capabilities Dirk was accepting Hendrik's offer.

'Good idea, Beit. You can do the routine tours of the territory while Georgie copes with surgery. It'd be a bit risky for her driving round alone, especially now the rains have come. She could get bogged down somewhere.'

Hendrik looked crestfallen, and Georgie guessed he had made his offer in the belief that they'd be working together.

It was a long day, not merely because of the volume of work, but because Georgie found herself agonising over Niklaas. She was certain that malaria could be very unpleasant. It was all very well for Dirk to play it down. He had his mother and several servants to wait on him if he succumbed. Surely someone should be looking after Niklaas? She was glad when the time came to close up the surgery for the day.

Hendrik had returned some little time before, eager for her to spend the evening with him. But she was adamant.

'No, thanks, not tonight. I'm whacked.' It wasn't altogether true. She was tired, but she also had to reassure herself as to Niklaas's welfare. 'But I'd be grateful if you'd drop me off at the bungalow.'

She entered the silent building, heading straight for Niklaas's bedroom. She took one appalled look, then, her fatigue forgotten, went into action.

Obviously the sick man had just thrown himself down fully clothed on to his unmade bed, where, judging by its dishevelled state, he had tossed and turned all day. A hand on his burning forehead was not really necessary to confirm that he was running a high fever, and when she spoke to him his eyes opened, resting on her in glazed incomprehension.

'Nik! Nik!' Urgently she shook his shoulder, finding his bush shirt clammy to the touch. 'Have you taken your medicine?'

Since no coherent reply was forthcoming, she began to look round for any signs of medication. There was nothing in the bedroom, but in the bathroom cabinet was a bottle which had not been touched for months, judging by the dust on the cap.

Tablets and a glass of water in hand, she advanced purposefully towards the bed, and Niklaas was in no state to resist her. The drug inside him beginning its work, she surveyed the exterior problem. One thing was certain, he couldn't be left in this state. There was no means of communication with the Lodge, and besides, she didn't think Niklaas would appreciate Dirk's help. She would have to cope.

First the bed. Half supporting, half dragging Niklass's heavy frame, Georgie managed to get him into a chair, then rapidly stripped and remade the bed. That was simple compared to her next task, one which tried her composure to the limits. Somehow she had to get Niklaas out of his sweat-soaked clothing. Look upon him as a patient, she told herself firmly. Forget that he's a man, it wasn't that she felt fear, as once she would have done at the sight of a male body, it was the effect of his physical attraction on her that she must ignore. His clothes stripped off, she pulled the covers over his nakedness with a shuddering sigh of relief.

But her ordeal wasn't over. To help bring down his temperature, he really ought to be sponged all over with tepid water. Doggedly she set about this, although her hands shook as if she too were possessed of a fever. She could not help but be aware of the magnificence of Niklaas's lean, muscular body, evenly bronzed all over. The red-brown hair on his chest tapered to a vee over his flat stomach and . . . she swallowed, forcing herself to maintain a clinical attitude, even while her hands longed to stray, to caress.

She'd been angry with him this morning, angry enough to walk out of his life, and she would have done it, if it hadn't been for this illness. And now? Now she knew she could never leave him, however intolerant, or intolerable, he might be. As she had tended him, it seemed as though a series of chemical explosions had taken place within her at the sight of him naked, yet strangely not vulnerable. Even in sickness he still exuded a potency that brought a searing response from her senses, disturbing her to the point of anguish.

The day had taken its toll, and so too had the physically draining emotions against which she had struggled, as she had cared for Niklaas. She was tired and hungry. He could safely be left for the short time it would take her to shower and eat.

She didn't intend to do so, but, having eaten her snack meal in the comfort of Niklaas's big armchair, she fell asleep, and did not wake until he disturbed her by stumbling on a frayed edge of carpet.

'Why did you leave me?' he demanded fretfully.

For a moment, Georgie stared at him, as he swayed in the doorway, wondering if this were an extension of her dream. For her sleep had been filled with tantalising visions of that bronzed, muscular body. But instead of sponging it, she had been running caressing fingers over its sinewy strength. In her dreams she too had been naked, and now, instinctively, she looked down, reassured to find herself securely wrapped in nightdress and robe.

Looking again at Niklaas, she realised he was in no fit condition to be wandering around. She sprang up, and an arm about his waist, one of his held across her shoulders, she urged him back to his room.

'Get back into bed, Nik,' she told him firmly, surprised when he obeyed so docilely. As she covered him, a fit of shivering racked his body.

'It's cold,' he complained.

'You'll soon be warm. You shouldn't have got up.'

'I wanted you,' he said simply. 'Don't leave me!'

'No, of course not. I'll be right here.' She pulled the chair close to the bed, but his head moved restlessly to and fro upon his pillows.

'That's no good. Hold me, darling, warm me.' He shivered again.

'I'll get some more blankets.'

'I don't *want* more blankets. It's human warmth I need. Do you know how long it is, my love, since somebody held me, warmed my body with theirs?'

Georgie thought she understood. It wasn't a physical chill he felt, but the need for comfort, tenderness, but Niklaas would never admit to such weakness. A longing engulfed her. What harm could there be in supplying such an innocent need?

'All right,' she murmured. She made to lie on the top of the bed, but he twitched the covers aside, pulling her down beside him with surprising strength. For a while she lay, holding herself tense, but he was so still that at last her courage returned and tentatively she put an arm about him, moved closer, trembling at her own daring.

His head turned on the pillow, his face only inches from hers.

'Stroke my body,' he commanded huskily, 'the way you were before.'

'I wasn't!' she denied. 'I was sponging you down, to lower your temperature.' She began to edge away, but a heavy arm restrained her.

'You raised it,' he murmured.

'Oh!' Georgie struggled indignantly. 'You knew all the time, and you let me think you were delirious!'

He didn't confirm or deny it.

'Stroke me,' he repeated, then, 'Kiss me, *love me*, sweetheart.' It was a deep groan of need.

'No! Let me go! I . . .'

'Then if you won't do it of your own free will, I'll have to make you. I'll make you need to touch me, make you want me!'

He wouldn't have to try very hard, Georgie thought, though she still fought to regain her liberty. Already she was on fire for him, scarcely surprising since her scantily clad body was imprisoned so tightly against the evidence of his arousal, the masculine scent of his fever-warmed body heady to her nostrils. He pulled her head nearer, so that her lips met his, the kiss a warm, searching statement of passionate need, kindling into flames the embers that burned already within her.

'Don't leave me, don't ever leave me again, my darling,' he murmured, his hands taking possession of her body, roaming over her, moulding her closer. 'Promise me?'

How could she leave him? Niklaas, the man she loved, when he seemed to need her so desperately?

'Tell me you're not in love with de Vries?'

'I've told you dozens of times, I'm not in love with Dirk,' she protested.

'He's never made love to you?'

'Of course not!'

'Do you love *me*?'

What a question. How was she to answer? Every

instinct urged her to say yes, but first there was something she had to tell him, and when he knew, would he still want her?

'Darling?' The tautness of his thighs, an extra tightening hardness, told her just how much he wanted her. She couldn't tell him now. Afterwards, she would tell him afterwards. She knew she could trust in his maturity, his essential goodness of nature, to understand that she couldn't be blamed for something that had happened so long ago, happened against her will.

'I love you, Niklaas,' she whispered. 'I *do* love you.'

They were both trembling, both bathed in sweat, his or hers? She didn't know. Their breathing was audible on the quiet, heavy night air. His hand's erotic exploration found its goal, and Georgie sobbed agonisingly in her throat as she fumbled, inexpertly at first, to return his caress. But he was patient, the to-and-fro glide of his skin against hers tormenting, tempting. Within her scorched fiery splinters of new sensations, of indescribable emotions, making her heart feel as though it must burst with the intensity of her feelings.

'Show me how much you love me,' he demanded, 'let me show you.'

Her response was a murmured 'yes', all she could manage, so restricted her breathing seemed to have become.

He rolled with her across the great double bed, raising himself to kneel over her. She trembled even more, but she was not afraid. Niklaas had banished fear. Instead she reached up, her arms about his waist, heard his gasp of pleasure as she received him, eagerly, willingly. But still he held back, stroking her inner thigh, making her cry out with intolerable longing.

'Are you sure? You're not afraid this time?'

'I'm sure, Nik, very sure. I love you, need you, *want* you!'

Then he moved against and within her, slowly, sensuously at first, then with increasing demand, her body responding joyously to his possession.

CHAPTER SEVEN

GEORGIE awoke to a chill sense of loss. She was lying in an empty bed. She sat up, then, although she was alone, flushed at the realisation of her own nakedness. But where was Niklaas? She discovered her nightdress and robe tangled among the sheets and hastily pulled them on.

A search of the bungalow soon revealed that she was alone. The jeep had gone too. She had forgotten to wind her watch last night, but returning to Niklaas's room she saw that his bedside clock showed only half-past seven. He must have left very early, and was he fit to be up and about his work? And if some emergency had arisen, why hadn't she heard Mugongo's summons? Why hadn't Niklaas woken her?

She showered and dressed, but had no appetite for breakfast. All she wanted was to see Niklaas, to assure herself of his well-being and to hear him repeat the words he had whispered last night during their lovemaking. And she had a duty to perform.

Last night there had been no opportunity to speak to him of her past, of the trauma which until now had inhibited her relationships with men. Following their lovemaking, Niklaas had not spoken again, but had fallen into a deep, uneasy sleep. Georgie had promised herself that in the morning, secure within the circle of his arms, safe in the knowledge of their shared love, she would make her confession.

Now she thought she could understand Niklaas's seemingly unreasonable moodiness, his silent disapproval of her dates with Dirk, his fury when he had discovered her, albeit innocently, in Hendrik's arms. Despite himself he had fallen in love again, with her. She gloried in the knowledge. The future looked marvellous, Georgie thought as she waited patiently on the veranda for Niklaas to return, for he would return for her as soon as he could, she knew.

It was an hour before she heard the sound of an engine, an hour which she had spent between daydreaming and rehearsing the words with which she would tell Niklaas about her past. As the sound of the vehicle grew nearer, she began to tremble with anticipation, a longing to see him, touch him, and unable to sit still she started to her feet, ran down the steps to meet him at the gate. But it was Hendrik who climbed down from the driving-seat.

'Morning, Georgie!' He gave her his normal cheerful greeting, but she thought he glanced warily at her. 'We knew you'd have no transport, so Dirk sent me to fetch you.'

'*Dirk* did? Oh.' She was disappointed. 'OK. I'll fetch my things.' Seated beside him, she asked, 'So Dirk knew Niklaas had had to go out early?'

Again Hendrik's expression puzzled her, but he nodded.

'I guessed something had come up,' she continued. 'Do you know what it was?'

'Georgie?' Hendrik not only looked but sounded puzzled now. 'Surely you must know why Niklaas left? I mean . . .'

'No, he left before I was awake. I suppose he was being considerate, didn't want to disturb me. But I wouldn't have minded.' She laughed happily, thinking just how little she would have objected to being woken by Niklaas.

Hendrik said no more, but the speed of his driving increased, and Georgie had to remind him of the restrictions.

'Sorry,' he said automatically, his thoughts apparently far away.

'Hendrik,' Georgie said at last, 'is something wrong?' Then she remembered that yesterday Niklaas had been ill and panic smote her. He was ill again? It hadn't just been malaria? But why hadn't he told her? Where was he? Had he been rushed to hospital? How? 'Hendrik!' she snapped his name out this time. 'There's something you're not telling me. You know where Niklaas is. You know what's happened. You *must* tell me!'

'I've no idea what happened, Georgie,' Hendrik said soberly. 'Only you know that. But it must have been one hell of a row.'

'What? What row? Who's had a row?'

'Well, you and Niklaas, obviously!'

Georgie struck a fist into the palm of her other hand.

'Niklaas and I did *not* have a row. I haven't the least idea what you're talking about.'

'Then I think you'd better wait until we get to the Lodge,' he suggested. 'Maybe Dirk can make sense out of all this. I certainly can't.'

'We're going to the Lodge, not the surgery? But I'll be late. Niklaas will be . . .'

'Niklaas isn't at the surgery, and,' anticipating her question, 'he isn't at the Lodge either. He's left.'

'Left? Left Marula, you mean?' Georgie willed the young scientist to say no, but he nodded. 'But

why would he do that? Where's he gone? How long
for?'

'Georgie, I told you, I don't know.'

A few moments later, she faced Dirk with the
same questions, her agitation increasing, and saw
the bewilderment in his face.

'I don't know why Niklaas left either. All I know
is where he's gone, and I know one other thing, that
he isn't coming back until you've left Marula.'

'What?' Georgie's legs began to shake, her
tongue cleaved to the roof of her mouth, so that she
was incapable of further speech.

'Georgie,' Dirk said gently, 'I think you'd better
sit down. You look awful. Now,' as she obeyed him,
'what can you tell me about this? I thought you and
Nik were getting on much better recently? Why
should he suddenly ask for your dismissal? It's hard
to think of any serious enough disagreements, and I
thought he was perfectly satisfied with your work.'
As she continued to stare at him disbelievingly, her
heart pounded a panic-stricken denial of his words.
Niklaas *couldn't* have asked for her dismissal, there
must be some mistake. 'Georgie? What happened?
You can tell me. Perhaps it's something that can be
put right.'

'I don't know, I just don't know.' But despite her
denial Georgie was beginning to think, with a
terrible sinking feeling, that she *did* know the
reason for Niklaas's precipitate departure. He was
regretting last night. That was all it could be.
Perhaps he hadn't been as coherent as she'd
thought. Perhaps his words, his lovemaking had
seemed like part of his delirium, until he'd woken
this morning and realised the truth. And then, she
thought bitterly, he hadn't been able to get away

fast enough. What a fool she'd been, to think that she had been capable of overcoming his prejudices. What had she thought was so special about her, that she had succeeded, where other women had failed, in erasing the memory of his wife's perfidy?

The two men were watching her anxiously, waiting for some explanation. She couldn't tell them the truth. All she had left to her now was her pride. Somehow her addled wits concocted a faltering story.

'There's only one thing it could have been,' she said, the words coming slowly, painfully. 'It's incredibly petty, but . . .' She swallowed. Even now, with the knowledge of Niklaas's certain rejection of her, it still hurt to denigrate him. 'It's petty,' she repeated, 'but he was still furious with me about the other night, when Hendrik and I got caught in the storm. He didn't believe, wouldn't believe that we hadn't . . . he feels very strongly about such things. And he accused me of letting my friendships with Hendrik and with you affect my work.'

To her surprise, Dirk didn't disagree with her. She'd been afraid he might dismiss her explanation as being feeble, unlikely.

'Hmm, yes. After what Lysette did to him. But it's no business of his what you do, unless . . .' Dirk's voice trailed away into thoughtfulness.

Despite her misery, Georgie was still capable of surprised conjecture. According to Hendrik, Dirk had been involved with Lysette, in her defection from her husband, yet here he was talking about it quite calmly, as if it had nothing to do with him. But she was too unhappy to indulge the curiosity she felt. One thing alone was certain, she must leave Marula. Niklaas wouldn't return whilst she stayed, and obviously Dirk couldn't afford to lose his chief veterinary. Besides, Marula was Niklaas's home. He had more right here than she did.

'If Hendrik will take me back to the bungalow I'll pack,' she said, though her lips trembled.

'No need for that just yet.'

'But I thought . . .'

'No, if you have to go, and I'm afraid I can't see any alternative, then at least you're entitled to a month's notice.' Dirk raised his hand as Georgie made a sound of protest. 'Niklaas has a backlog of leave owing to him. He rarely took a holiday. He's decided to take that leave whilst you work out your notice.'

Perhaps Dirk would prefer such an arrangement to paying her a month's wages in lieu, and Georgie didn't want money for services she hadn't performed, she thought proudly.

'All right. If you're sure he won't be coming back, before . . .' Her voice very nearly cracked at the thought of leaving Marula, the place she had come to love, at the thought of not seeing Niklaas again. Forever was a long time.

'You have my assurance. He's said he's taking six weeks. That's the Christmas period and well into the New Year. I've asked for Hendrik to be seconded to us for that length of time. Once you've left, he can carry on alone for the couple of weeks until Niklaas gets back.'

It wasn't easy, living alone in Niklaas's bungalow, working in his surgery, when both places held so many poignant memories. One place she never entered, his bedroom, the place of betrayal. For that was how it felt. Finally she had learnt to trust a man, and now it seemed he had no more integrity than Ralph. *Had* it been delirium that had made Niklaas give in, perhaps unwittingly, to his physical cravings? If she could only believe that, it would mean he wasn't utterly despicable.

Having Hendrik's company helped a little, but only by day, when she could lose herself in professionalism, even laugh occasionally at one of his quips. Dirk too was as attentive as ever, and in a mood of reckless unhappiness she accepted his invitations, even, occasionally, enduring the society of Reita de Vries. Anything rather than spend empty hours in useless longing.

Night was the worst time. Sometimes, if she was lucky, she went to bed so tired that she slept heavily, if unrefreshingly, but there were many white nights when she lay, eyes wide open, seeing, not her surrounding, but pictures of Niklaas, superimposed upon wall and ceiling.

But her month's notice was expiring rapidly. Another three or four days, and she would be leaving Marula for ever. Though the thought brought tears to her eyes, the bulk of her packing was already done, and she had written to her parents, warning them that her return was imminent.

Once she was back in England, she reassured herself, it would be easier to forget, and with a return of her spirits her appetite would improve. She knew she was losing too much weight, but the sultry heat and her unhappiness combined to make her feel nauseous at the very sight of food. It was foolish, of course, she should make more effort to eat, but somehow it didn't seem to matter very much, even though she was aware that her work was beginning to suffer, her tasks often performed automatically with a general sense of malaise.

And then, one morning, three days before Christmas, after a particularly gruelling operation, Georgie fainted. She had no forewarning, did not realise what had happened to her, until she regained consciousness at the Lodge and found Hendrik and Dirk leaning over her.

Despite her protests, Dirk insisted on radioing for a doctor, a flying service based in Johannesburg, insisted too that she should stay at the Lodge until a diagnosis had been made.

'You've been overdoing things,' he told her. 'Just because I haven't said anything it doesn't mean I haven't noticed. You're deliberately driving yourself, and you're unhappy. You don't want to leave Marula, do you?'

She shook her head, tears of weakness springing to her eyes.

'I love it here,' she whispered.

'You don't have to leave,' Dirk said slowly, 'if it means that much to you. There is a way you could stay.'

Georgie stared at him uncomprehendingly. How could she stay when Niklaas had said she must go? He would refuse to work with her. Perhaps it was because she felt so ill that her wits were slow. But Dirk was not given an opportunity to explain. Reita de Vries, having been advised of Georgie's presence, her illness, appeared in the living-room, making it quite plain that she didn't intend Georgie and her son to be left alone together, and despite Dirk's diffident suggestion that his mother must have things to do, that he could perfectly well keep Georgie company until the doctor arrived, Reita

was not to be moved. And, though she didn't care
for Dirk's mother, Georgie was almost glad of her
presence, the virtual silence it imposed. She was
busy with her own thoughts, remembering, making
calculations. And she was right. When the doctor
arrived, some hours later, it didn't need his
confirmation to tell her what she had already
guessed. She was pregnant. She was carrying
Niklaas's child. For a brief instant there was
exultation, followed at once by crushing despair.

Suddenly all Georgie wanted to do was to get
away, suddenly she needed the reassurance only her
mother could give her. She *couldn't* carry this
burden alone, here among strangers. In tears, she
begged Dirk to take her back to the bungalow, to
collect her things, to take her to Johannesburg, the
first step on her journey home.

'I shan't be well enough to work out my notice
anyway. The doctor said . . .'

'Why?' Dirk asked sharply. 'What's wrong with
you? What did he say, Georgie? There's nothing
seriously wrong with you, is there?' His face was
paler than usual, green eyes full of genuine concern.

Out of courtesy, Reita de Vries had been forced to
speed the doctor's departure, but she would not be
absent for long, and then Dirk's opportunity to
question her would be gone. He must have realised
this, for he agreed to take Georgie back to the
bungalow. But on the way she realised the reason
for his easily won compliance.

'Now!' He stopped the Land Rover in a clearing,
halfway between Lodge and bungalow. 'I want to
know exactly what's wrong with you. We don't
move another inch until you tell me, and I certainly
won't help you to get to Johannesburg, not without

knowing everything. For one thing, I don't think you're fit to travel.'

For an instant, Georgie considered lying, but what was the point? She needed desperately to get away, but she also needed to confide in someone. Her mother was some days beyond her reach. With a calmness of which she hadn't thought herself capable, she told Dirk everything.

She did not even omit the trauma of Ralph, how finally it had been overcome, and now this. As she spoke she avoided his gaze, but then, at the end of her story, she turned to face him, stony-eyed in her misery. It was the compassion in his face that was her undoing, and he gathered her into his arms as she wept, totally unable to control her tattered emotions.

When at last she was quiet, a silence broken by spasmodic sobs, Dirk spoke. It was as if he had been thinking carefully during her wild outburst of grief.

'You're in love with Niklaas.' It wasn't a question. She'd already admitted as much.

'Yes,' the word was a choked whisper, then, more strongly, 'but he must never know. He obviously despises me for letting him, and he must never know about the child.'

'No,' Dirk agreed thoughtfully. 'That wouldn't be a good idea right now. Have you thought,' he continued, 'what you'll do? You weren't considering an abortion?'

'Heavens, no!' Georgie said indignantly. 'I'll go home, have the baby and just hope that my parents . . .' her voice cracked as she thought longingly of Maggie and Paul, 'hope they'll understand. At least afterwards I'll still have my profession. I'll be able to keep myself and the child.'

'There is an alternative, Georgie,' Dirk said carefully, deliberately unemotional. 'You could marry someone else. At least your child would have a name. It would be less upsetting for your family. Then they need never know. It would be better for the child, later on.'

'There isn't anyone,' Georgie said flatly. 'Besides, even if there were . . .'

'There's me. No, don't say anything yet. You must know I'm in love with you. I've never said anything, because you didn't seem to want me to, I realise why now. At first I thought it was young Beit, but of course,' he sighed heavily, 'it was Niklaas.'

Georgie was touched.

'Dirk, I know you mean it kindly, but I . . . The thought of marriage to anyone else—it wouldn't . . . I couldn't . . .' She broke off, shivering.

'It would be in name only,' Dirk interrupted hastily. 'I realise I couldn't ask any more of you. I wouldn't ask.'

'No. That wouldn't be fair to you. What would you get out of it? Nothing!'

'At least I'd have the pleasure of knowing you were my wife, of seeing you every day, instead of knowing that I'd never see you again,' Dirk spoke painfully. 'You must know how that idea feels?'

'Yes,' Georgie whispered, 'but how would I stand it, seeing Niklaas?'

'You needn't see him. You know he never willingly crosses my threshold, and we could travel too. I could show you other parts of South Africa, places just as lovely as Marula.'

Georgie shook her head. Nowhere could ever

compare with Marula. But—she stopped—wasn't that because Marula held Niklaas, because here she had fallen in love, finally shaken off a fear that had haunted her for years. And what had she gained instead? she asked herself bitterly. She'd only exchanged a haunted mind for a haunted heart and tormented body.

'I couldn't, Dirk. It wouldn't be right or fair, to any of us. It would be impossible to avoid Niklaas for ever, and even if I could he'd find out I was still here.'

And then he'd believe he'd been right all along, that it was Dirk she'd been after, that, like Lysette, she'd preferred the owner to the employee, that, like Lysette and Reita, her motives were mercenary. But why should she care what Niklaas thought? It wouldn't matter to him.

'And then there's your mother,' she remembered.

'Damn and blast my mother!' Dirk exploded with a violence of which she hadn't believed him capable. 'She's always ruled my life. Until now I didn't really care, because there was nothing I wanted badly enough to oppose her. But I'm determined on this. I want to marry you, Georgie, and if my mother doesn't like it, she can leave Marula. My father's will provided her with a perfectly adequate annual allowance, but if necessary I'll supplement it. She could even go and live with Lysette.' He laughed ironically. 'They always got on well together. I think she was the only woman my mother would have welcomed as my wife.'

'Lysette. You don't mean Niklaas's *wife*?' There must be some mistake.

'Of course!'

'But I thought she was dead.'

'Good lord, whatever gave you that idea? Oh no, dear Lysette is still very much alive. In fact, Niklaas mentioned that he'd be looking her up while he's down at the Cape.'

Pain stabbed through Georgie. Niklaas's wife was alive, and it seemed he had never stopped loving her, in spite of everything. Why otherwise would he be visiting her? Perhaps, in his delirium, he'd even imagined that *she* was Lysette. Now that she thought about it, she couldn't recall Niklaas calling her by name.

'Niklaas gave me the impression that she was dead,' Georgie said grimly. An impression? Yes. But he hadn't actually said the words. Had she assumed, wanted to think . . .?

'Why would he do that?'

'I don't know,' Georgie said slowly, and she didn't. There had been no reason for Niklaas to deceive her. 'Maybe I just misunderstood.'

It wasn't just the knowledge that Lysette was still alive and that, Dirk told her, she and Niklaas had never been divorced, that made Georgie reconsider Dirk's offer of marriage. There was a mail delivery the next day, and amongst it several Christmas cards for her. The card from her parents enclosed a letter from Paul Jonson.

'You're not to worry,' he wrote, 'but your mother has been extremely ill. She wouldn't let me tell you before. She's quite recovered now, but the doctors recommend a long period of convalescence with no strain or worry, and above all a warmer climate. So I decided to take a slightly earlier retirement than originally planned. I've sold the practice and I'm taking Maggie to Australia, so that she doesn't have to endure our winter.'

In a postscript, he added that they had received Georgie's letter, telling them of her intention to return home.

'I'm sorry about that, love, but I've been in touch with your Mother's Aunt Esme and she'll be delighted to put you up, until we come back and settle where we're going to live.'

Georgie had never met Esme Dane, her great-aunt, but she felt sure, being of an older, more strictly reared generation, that her great-aunt would not be so welcoming towards a niece who was pregnant and unmarried.

Dirk was touchingly delighted when she told him of her decision.

'You'll never regret it, Georgie, I promise, and if anything should ever happen to me, you'll be all right. Marula will be yours, your home and the child's.'

At his words, Georgie felt a pang of guilt. She was receiving so much, giving so little. She could try, she thought, to be a good wife to Dirk. Perhaps later on, after the birth of her child, when time had done its healing work, she might be able to bring herself to ... It was as if Dirk had read her mind, for he repeated his earlier promise.

'I shan't ask anything of you, Georgie, anything that you're unwilling to give. If the time ever comes when you feel any affection for me, I'll leave it to you to say the word.'

To Georgie's utter amazement, Reita de Vries did not make one of her usual attempts to ride roughshod over her son. She seemed to accept his determination to marry with equanimity, and agreed to his suggestion of an increased allowance and that she should make her permanent home elsewhere.

'My mother knows about you being pregnant, Georgie,' Dirk said, amazing her still further. 'She'd guessed in any case. She's a very astute woman. But I let her think the child was young Beit's. I thought you'd prefer that? The fewer people who know the truth . . .'

'Wouldn't it have been better to let her think it was yours?'

'Er—no, not really. I think it's better this way, believe me.'

They were married quietly, in the New Year, in Johannesburg, with only the two statutory witnesses. Georgie wrote a brief note to the forwarding address her stepfather's letter had included, telling her parents of her change of plans, her marriage. She didn't expect to hear from them for some while, and, when she did, she would be able to tell them quite naturally the news that they were to be grandparents.

Life at Marula assumed an even tenor, and though she was by no means happy Georgie strove for inner tranquillity for the sake of the child she carried and for the outward appearance of it for the sake of her husband. Dirk, despite an occasional expression of wistfulness, never betrayed his feelings, or attempted to break his word, and while they were not, would never be, lovers, they were becoming increasingly good friends, and she felt she knew him well enough to question him about Lysette.

'Were you ever in love with her?'

'No,' said Dirk with a positiveness that couldn't be disbelieved. 'And she wasn't in love with me. I doubt if she's capable of loving anyone except herself. Her infatuation with Niklaas didn't last long, once she'd discovered his job wasn't as romantic as she'd supposed, that he wasn't a wealthy man.'

'So why did you . . .'

'Associate with her?' Dirk gave a short laugh. 'That was entirely my mother's idea. She and Lysette were kindred spirits. Mother was always inviting her to the Lodge, to accompany us on our travels. She hoped that, if Niklaas divorced Lysette, she'd marry me and that we'd all be one big happy family, that I'd agree to leave the Lodge and live permanently in Jo'burg or Cape Town. Lysette was willing enough, but I wasn't, though I couldn't convince Nik that I wasn't a party to their plans.' He sounded regretful, and Georgie believed him, when he said he deplored the enmity Niklaas bore him. 'We were such good pals when we were kids. I wasn't fit enough, of course, to keep up with all old Nik's activities, but he was very patient with a sickly kid most of the time. He got on well with my father too.' Georgie could tell that Dirk would have liked to experience the same rapport with Klaus de Vries. Instead, he had been tied to his mother's apron strings.

It was mid-January when Georgie learnt that
Niklaas was home. She found out when Hendrik
called to make his farewells.

'Van der Walt is back, so this is goodbye.' He
hesitated, but as Dirk was not present he continued,
'I was surprised when you married de Vries. I knew
you were never interested in me in that way, of
course, but I did think you and Niklaas ...'
Deliberately, Georgie exhibited calm surprise, and
he shrugged. 'Oh well, just shows, you never can
tell. But that time he hit me, I could've sworn ...'

Dirk was reassuring. There was no earthly
reason, he told Georgie, why she should encounter
Niklaas. Marula was a big spread, and these days
she never went near the surgery. Niklaas hadn't set
foot in the Lodge since before his separation from
Lysette.

But no one was predictable, she discovered,
Niklaas least of all, and he did come to the Lodge,
deliberately seeking her out.

CHAPTER EIGHT

DIRK had gone to Cape Town. Just a short visit, he had told Georgie, for a routine check on his own health. He hadn't suggested that she should accompany him, and she was relieved. She was suffering badly from morning sickness, and felt that the journey to Johannesburg, the flight to the Cape, might be too much for her.

She didn't mind being alone at the Lodge. She loved the graciously proportioned rooms, the delightful views from every window, and already she had begun to impose her own personality upon the house, something with which Reita de Vries had never troubled. Marula Lodge lacked only one thing to make it perfect. If only it could have been Niklaas who shared it with her!

She was dreaming thus over a book, the contents of whose pages she was not absorbing, when the black maid announced a visitor.

'Missus de Vries, Mr Nik'las here!'

'Oh no!' Involuntarily the words escaped her lips as, hard upon the maid's heels, Niklaas entered the living-room, not looking to right or left, but bearing down directly upon Georgie where she sat.

'Surprised to see me?' he said tautly. 'Not a pleasant surprise, I imagine?'

'What are you doing here?' she demanded. 'You *never* come to the Lodge. You . . .'

'Not if I can possibly avoid it, but in the last two months I've been forced to come here twice, both times because of *you*!'

'You don't need to be here now. Please leave!' Georgie stood up, very much the outraged chatelaine dismissing an unwanted guest.

'Oh yes, I do, because I need to tell you just what I think of you. That way, maybe, I'll be able to get you out of my system.'

'You've already made your feelings pretty clear,' Georgie retorted, 'when you demanded that Dirk dismiss me!'

'What?' Niklaas actually looked taken aback, but he recovered swiftly. 'I don't know what the hell you're talking about. All I do know is that you're a liar, a cheat, and promiscuous to boot. First young Beit, then . . . *Why* did you let me make love to you, Georgie, when you knew all along you intended to marry Dirk?'

'But I didn't . . .' Georgie began indignantly.

'Didn't he ever ask you for an explanation?'

'Yes,' Georgie said defiantly, 'and I gave him one. I told him everything.'

'And yet he married you. Bloody fool. Damn me if I can decide which of you is the worst. You could have told me, instead of letting me go off on a wild goose chase.'

'But we didn't know before, and what wild goose chase? I don't understand.'

'Don't make things worse! I can just imagine the pair of you sitting here cosily, laughing at my expense. After all those years of refusing to divorce Lysette, I go haring down to Cape Town like a madman to set the wheels in motion so that I can marry *you* because, poor deluded fool that I was, I thought you were different!'

Georgie sat down heavily, her face white, beads

of perspiration standing out on her forehead.

'Niklaas,' she could hardly speak for the way her tongue cleaved drily to the roof of her mouth, 'would you please explain, calmly and slowly, just what *did* happen the morning you went away?'

'As if you didn't know,' he said scornfully, 'but all right. I'll spell it out for you. It will do me good to watch your face, to see you trying to act a lie and failing. I only wish de Vries were here—I'd like to punch him on the nose. I may still do that.' Niklaas paused, taking a deep breath. 'That night you came to me I knew, realised when it was too late, that you were no virgin.'

'I never said I was!' Georgie cried. 'You assumed. I was going to tell you, to explain . . .'

'You didn't need to.' Niklaas was moving restlessly about the room, picking up the little items with which Georgie had brought it alive, native carvings, hand-sewn patchwork. 'I knew you'd slept with Hendrik.'

'But I . . .'

'I also knew it was only the once, and I felt it was partly my fault that he'd been able to seduce you so easily. After all, you were ripe for love, for me, or so I thought, and I'd rejected you. And in any case, I couldn't condemn you for what you'd done. At least I'm not guilty of double standards. Against my will I'd fallen in love with you, but I was still married. I got up early, came here and told Dirk I wanted to take some leave,' bitterly, 'I even told him why. Damn you to hell, Georgie! My divorce proceedings are under way and I come back here to tell you, only to find that it was Dirk all along, or, at least, it was Marula. You were always saying how much you loved it, how much you wanted to live here always. I was fool enough to think you were trying to convince me, that you wanted to be with me. But now you're married to Dirk, Marula *is* yours, isn't it, yours and your heirs'? I presume you do intend to give Dirk an heir?'

Georgie didn't, couldn't, answer him. Her thoughts were in an utter turmoil, her emotions too. Dirk had lied to her. Why? He couldn't have been certain that she'd marry him on the rebound. There had to be some reason. The feud between Niklaas and Dirk couldn't have been as one-sided as Dirk had pretended.

And Niklaas loved her. Had loved her, she corrected herself. All he felt for her now was scorn and hatred. And it was no use telling him Dirk had lied. He wouldn't believe her. Why should he, when he was so ready to credit her with other falsehoods? But she couldn't bear his presence any longer. She was on the verge of breaking down. Niklaas mustn't witness her disintegration, and she had to be alone, to think.

'You've had your say. Please go now.' A precarious calm made her voice cold, indifferent.

'Yes. But that wasn't all I came for. Before I go . . .' He moved so swiftly that she had no time to cry out for assistance, though it was doubtful if any of the servants would have heard or, if they had, dared to interfere. His arms clamped round her, forcing her up against him, his arousal not of love but of frustrated anger. His lips, his teeth ground against hers and she tasted salt—her own blood, or the tears that coursed down her cheeks?

Savagely, insultingly, his hands were contouring her body, but, even though she knew his mood was one of revenge, she felt an inner stirring, a painful

longing that had never really subsided. But as
involuntarily she moved against him, parted her
lips to him, her hands beginning to slide over his
shoulders, seeking the nape of his neck, he thrust
her roughly away.

'Oh no, you don't! My God, Georgie, what kind
of woman are you? You want it all, don't you? Dirk,
Marula and me too.' Niklaas stared at her, his face
contorted with loathing, before he turned and
strode from the room, the sound of banging doors
reverberating long after he had left and long after
Georgie had collapsed in an agony of misery.

It had been too late to take action then, but thank
God Dirk was away for several days. When finally
she regained her self-control, Georgie was able to
plan, and the next day she had one of the drivers
take her to Johannesburg. It was a long journey, and
she was mortally afraid of what the uncomfortable,
sometimes jerky, ride might do to her, or to the child
within her.

'How long will you be in Jo'burg, Mrs de Vries?'
her driver asked. 'Do you want me to stay over, to
drive you back?'

'No, thanks. I'm not quite sure when I'll be back,'
Georgie lied. She had no intention of returning to
Marula, ever. 'I'll radio in when I want to be picked
up.'

Cocooned in a lethargic numbness of spirit,
Georgie scarcely noticed the details of her flight
home, her overnight stay in London, her journey to
Esme Dane's East Anglian home. A telephone call
had brought forth a delighted invitation to come
and stay for as long as she liked.

And she had stayed for two years. Aunt Esme had

been kind and surprisingly understanding about Georgie's 'broken marriage'.

'I'm glad I never married, my dear. Men can be such brutes.'

The arrangement had worked very well. Esme was happy to have company, and Georgie was grateful for a home in which to bring up little Susan. Although she had visited her parents when, finally, they returned to Yorkshire, she had decided that it was safer to remain with Esme Dane, even though it was unlikely that Dirk would come in search of her. He must be aware that she knew the truth, how he had deceived her. What was it Paul Jonson had said, when she'd described Dirk de Vries as being 'a pussycat'? 'Cats have claws,' he'd said. Dirk's had remained sheathed for a long time, but finally they had done their damage, to her and to Niklaas.

If she had been blessed with the gift of clairvoyance, Georgie would never had left her great-aunt's cottage that morning, but it would only have postponed and not avoided the eventual, fateful encounter.

As it was, ignorant of impending events, she opened the front door, catching her breath as the icy air assailed her lungs. The strong east wind made it quite a hard task to pull the door closed behind her. Then, her silvery head protected by the hood of her duffle coat, she thrust mittened hands deep down into its pockets and made her way as quickly as was safe down the slippery, snow-bound path. Huge, purposeful snowflakes were still falling. This had been a particularly hard winter. Many people had fallen and injured themselves, including her great-aunt, now in hospital.

Looking about her, Georgie thought it hardly seemed possible that this was the same garden where she had worked in spring and summer, fighting the ever-advancing weeds, deliberately urging on her tired body, so that at night her brain might find ease in forgetfulness.

It was hard to imagine her summer self, her slender body clad in shorts and sleeveless T-shirt, when now, to survive the East Anglian winter, it was necesssary to be muffled to the eyebrows. Harder still to believe that, just two years ago, winter and the fast-approaching season of Christmas had been spent in very different surroundings, a very different climate, where December was an outrageously warm and balmy month.

Marula! She fought down the almost unbearable nostalgia that rose in her. Marula was the past, a past she had voluntarily abandoned.

Still carefully choosing her steps, Georgie made her way towards the small village, which boasted only a public house, a church and a few shops, just sufficient for the immediate needs of its residents. For any more complicated shopping, it was necessary to go into the nearest town.

But despite its limitations, its isolation, she was happy here living with Aunt Esme—or, she qualified, happier than she had ever expected to be again. At least life here was free from strife. She was, she had persuaded herself, content to remain here, and if she missed the challenge of her former profession, if there were absent other elements that her vital nature craved, she had learnt to suppress the need, for Susan's sake.

With the impatient gesture of one who thrusts aside an unpleasant memory, she tucked away an errant strand of the blonde hair which had escaped the hood of her coat and stepped out more briskly.

Her few purchases were swiftly made, but it took some time and tact to extricate herself from the inquisition of the shopkeepers and acquaintances, all of whom knew Esme Dane well and must enquire after her injury, ask after Georgie's own welfare and after that of small Susan, who was a universal favourite in the neighbourhood.

'She's much better,' said Georgie, her thin, intelligent face lighting up with affection, as it always did when she thought or spoke of her tiny daughter. 'But I've left her with next door. She still has a nasty cough, and I didn't want to risk bringing her out in this biting wind. I'll be glad when the better weather comes.'

The wool shop was her last call, where she collected another two ounces of the pale pink wool her aunt was using to knit a cardigan for Susan. Georgie had promised to take in the wool when she visited Esme the following afternoon.

As she left the shop, she collided painfully with a tall figure that hindered her departure. With words of apology on her lips, Georgie looked up, ready for a humorous exchange about mutual clumsiness. Like the December air, the words chilled on her lips. It seemed, too, as if the cold had affected her lungs, as searing pain assailed her chest.

This had been no awkward blunder, but a deliberate barring of her way. The soft, snow-muffled sounds of village life, her surroundings, vanished into a numb void as, blue eyes widened with shock, she stared up into the strong features she had never expected to see again, had persuaded herself she didn't *want* to see again. Now, in this

suspended moment of time, she knew just what a
self-delusion that had been.

As far as Georgie was concerned, they might
have stood there forever transfixed, encapsulated in
a bubble of silence, but he spoke.

'So, I've found you at last.'

'Niklaas!' Her lips barely managed the soundless
formation of his name. Neither of them was aware
of other shoppers brushing past. Her legs began to
shake, her thoughts to pursue each other on an
endless merry-go-round of conjecture. How had he
found her? Her parents had promised not to reveal
her whereabouts to anyone. And now that he had
found her, how was she to escape him again? She
was uncomfortably aware that his vivid green eyes
were making a thorough inspection of her, not that
he could discern much of her figure or appearance
in the all-enveloping duffle coat and hood. He
continued to stare assessingly, and certain that, as
usual, he was finding something in her to criticise,
she tilted her sharp chin at him, her blue eyes now
coldly hostile, as she tried to quell the unreasonable,
unruly behaviour of her heart. Niklaas meant
absolutely nothing to her, not any more, and she
wasn't going to give him any reason to think
otherwise. She steeled herself to hold his glance.

'What are *you* doing here?'

His eyes held a mocking glint. He hadn't missed
the nervous edge to her voice or the way her hands
fidgeted with the paper bag she held. He made her
wait for an answer while, with fingers whose steely
strength she remembered all too well, he steered her
away from the congested doorway, away from the
reassuring presence of other people. Even though,
just an instant ago, she had been telling herself that

Niklaas was part of a past with which she could well dispense, at the first touch of his hand on her arm her nerves tingled, belying the assertion.

In that instant, Georgie was aware of many emotions. A heart-tugging remembrance of what had been, of what might have been, but principally she was aware of fear, fear that he might discover the secret she had been hiding for the past two years. There was anger, too. It seemed that he had deliberately tracked her down, since by no stretch of the imagination could this meeting be coincidence. Niklaas, who disliked leaving Marula, was a long way from home. Why had he to come back into her life, just as she had achieved a comparative tranquillity?

'Georgie!' The deep voice, whose accent had always fascinated her, was commanding her attention. He sounded irritated, his grip of her upper arms intensified. Dully she responded.

'How did you find me? Why should you *want* to find me?' He hadn't tried to follow her, obviously hadn't been concerned about her destination or welfare, when she'd left Marula almost exactly two years ago. She looked up into the stern ascetic features, at the inscrutable bronzed face that looked so startlingly out of place in this snow-covered English village street.

The amused glint had long since left his eyes, their green had become that of ice-bound seas, and she remembered—as if she had ever forgotten!— how chilling his anger could be. But his tone was edgy rather than angry.

'I didn't want to find you, I had to find you. How doesn't matter. Suffice it that I have.' He released her arms now that he had her full attention, and thrusting hands into pockets, he leant against the churchyard wall. Obviously he intended the conversation to be a protracted one.

Georgie had no such intention. Apart from the fact that it was cold, that Susan became troubled if she was gone too long, she had no wish to hold any kind of conversation with Niklaas. It annoyed her, after all her efforts to forget, that every move, every expression of his was as familiar to her as if their last meeting had been only yesterday.

'Well, Georgie. Now you can tell me why you ran away. You were never a coward, but that's what you did. You told no one you were going, or where, or why.'

No, she wasn't a coward, except where Niklaas was concerned, and now his questions, his probing glance, were arousing the familiar sensations of panic, panic that urged her to flight.

It was futile, she knew, hopeless to think that she could escape him. With his long legs he was fleeter of foot than she, even if the ground surface had not been so treacherous. Nevertheless, she turned and fled, away from the village, away from him, making for the place that represented sanctuary, her aunt's cottage. How she kept her balance she didn't know, as she ran like a madwoman, her booted feet slipping and sliding on the perilously frozen snow. Her progress on the encrusted surface was noisy, yet she could hear him in pursuit, hear his shouted commands to her to stop, his muffled curses as he too fought an unequal battle with the icy ground. Fought, but lost.

Georgie heard an imprecation uttered louder than the rest, and the sharp sound as of a twig cracking underfoot. Despite her inner agitation, the need to watch her step, an uneasy intuition made her turn, turn to see Niklaas stretched out upon the frozen ground, one leg oddly twisted under him.

'Oh, my God!' Horrified, no longer concerned with her own safety, she began to stumble back towards him. All she could think of now was that he was hurt and that it was her fault. She could have parted from him in a more dignified manner, made it quite clear with a few well-chosen words that she wanted nothing to do with him, that this had been a wasted journey. But instead, like a gauche school-girl, she had fled, and Niklaas, who could never bear to be bested, had followed.

Her shopping dropped unheeded in the snow, as she knelt by his side, her eyes anxiously scanning the face that was suddenly as grey as the tramped background against which it lay, lines of pain drawn from nose to mouth twisted in silent anguish.

'Nik, are you——? Is it——?'

'Yes, damn you!' he managed from between clenched teeth. 'I am hurt, and yes, it probably is broken and what the bloody hell do you care?' Niklaas had always been inclined to swear when angered, but this time it was pain which lent an added violence to his tone. 'Go on!' he said bitterly, 'run away, blast you! You're safe. I can't catch you now.'

'Stay there!' she said, knowing immediately how ridiculously inane her words sounded. Usually cool and efficient in moments of crisis, the fact that this was Niklaas lying injured had paralysed her faculties.

'I promise you I shan't stir an inch!' For a moment there was a touch of the wry humour that once she had relished so much, and deep within her sudden pain wrenched, pain that was a sense of loss.

'I'll cover you with my coat,' she began to remove it.

'For heaven's sake, woman, don't dither. Keep your blasted coat on and fetch that help you mentioned. I suppose there *is* assistance to be had in this benighted hole?'

As Georgie looked around her, uncertain for a moment whether to go or stay, aid arrived in the shape of two farm-workers on their way home to lunch, and fortunately it didn't take the men long to assess the situation.

'Broken something, has he? Best if we carry him into your cottage, Miss Jonson.' She saw Niklaas's eyes narrow at this form of address.

'Oh, but . . .'

'It's the nearest place,' the same man pointed out. 'Best to get him into the warm and phone for the doctor. Poor old doc, he's had a busy time of it these past weeks, what with broken limbs.'

Swiftly Georgie weighed pros and cons. She didn't want Niklaas at the cottage for various reasons, but it would appear very strange if she refused to succour someone she obviously knew, and it would only be for a short while. As soon as Dr Grey arrived, Niklaas would be whisked off to the hospital. If she could just persuade Susan to stay next door a little longer she might avoid her most pressing problem, explanation of the child's existence.

'All right, bring him in. I'll run on ahead and telephone.' And arrange things with next door, she thought.

Burdened by Niklaas's not inconsiderable weight, the men were unable to move very fast, so that a somewhat breathless Georgie was able to meet them at the door with at least the appearance of calm, the knowledge that for the moment she was safe from discovery.

'Put him on the couch there. The doctor's out on a call at the moment,' she told Niklaas, 'but they're trying to contact him.'

Obviously considering they had fulfilled their Samaritan obligations, the men departed and Georgie was left looking doubtfully at her unwanted visitor.

'Would you like me to take a look at your leg?' she asked. Instinctively her training prompted her to help, but knowledge of her own vulnerability made her reluctant to touch him.

'No!' His face was a mask of ill-concealed pain. 'You may be an excellent vet, but since I'm neither a domesticated nor a wild animal, I prefer to wait until the doctor arrives.'

If they'd been in the bush he'd have had to accept her help, Georgie thought, remembering how they had operated on the wounded Mugongo. But trust Niklaas, even though in great discomfort, to work in a jibe at her profession. He hadn't really taken her chosen line of work seriously after all, she brooded.

'But a good stiff drink would be appreciated,' he broke in upon her thoughts.

'We don't keep alcohol in the house,' she told him, 'and even if we did I don't think you should. I could give you a cup of tea, or coffee?'

'I'll settle for the tea,' his aquiline nose wrinkled, 'I remember your coffee . . . vividly. But you said "we". Who else lives here, since I gather you've reverted to your maiden name?'

'Just myself and my aunt,' she told him, fingers crossed behind her back. Please, please let Susan go on playing happily with the child next door. When Susan suddenly decided she wanted her mother and no one else, there was no pacifying her.

'Do I get to meet your aunt?'

'No!' abruptly, then unwillingly: 'She's in hospital. She fell too, a couple of days ago, but at her age it's a lot more serious.' Thank goodness Niklaas and Esme never would meet.

'So you're here on your own?' His eyes were suddenly speculative.

'Yes . . . no . . . that is . . .'

'Got a friend staying while Auntie's away? Is that it? Same old Georgie—must have a man in tow.'

On the point of furious repudiation, Georgie hesitated. It might be a good idea to let him think she did have a boy-friend available. But on the other hand she hated deception, and to utter this particular untruth would be to give herself a sordid image which, despite Niklaas's opinion of her, she did not warrant.

'Not staying. But I get plenty of visitors.'

'I bet!'

Georgie clenched her teeth, recognising the implication behind the deliberate stress he laid on the simple words. She had removed her duffle coat now, and he was treating her face and figure to a comprehensive appraisal, subtly insulting.

'You haven't changed much,' he said, his inspection complete, by which time Georgie's face and neck were peony pink. 'You've put on a bit of weight, perhaps, but it suits you. You were inclined to be scraggy before.'

'Thank you very much! I could say the same for

you. You haven't changed either. You're still as . . .
as . . . oh . . .' She turned on her heel. 'I'll get you
that cup of tea.' Her expressive face told him she
hoped it choked him, and he read the message.

'Don't put too much arsenic in it,' he called after
her. 'I believe quite a small amount is sufficiently
lethal!'

How could he joke, when he must be in the most
dreadful pain? But then Niklaas was no weakling,
far from it. She brewed the tea, taking care to make
it the way he liked it, strong and sweet. Georgie
smiled drily to herself as she thought of his remark
about the arsenic, and wished that instead she could
have slipped in some barbiturate or other, just
enough to make him doze off until the doctor
arrived, just enough to stop him from quizzing her
about the last two years. Niklaas liked to call the
shots. He would never be satisfied with just having
found her. Deliberately she didn't hurry back to the
living-room, but at last she could put off the
moment no longer, and carried through the tray
bearing two mugs of tea.

He looked as alert as ever, though it was obvious
his pain had not diminished, and now she found
herself wishing that the doctor would arrive, not
only to relieve her, but to ease Niklaas's discomfort.
Even after all the pain he had caused her, she
couldn't be vindictive enough to gloat over his
present predicament.

'Working locally, are you?' Niklaas asked as she
handed him his mug, careful as she did so not to let
her fingers brush his. 'Shouldn't have thought
there'd be much scope for a practice round here. A
bit limited after what you've been used to.'

'I haven't worked since I came back to England,' she told him.

'Really?' Dark, demonic brows arched in surprise. 'That doesn't sound like you. I thought you were a fanatical career woman. Wasn't that why you ran out on your marriage? Been ill?' He fired the questions sharply. As if, she thought cynically, he could ever feel concern for her health.

'I'm perfectly well, thank you, but Aunt Esme isn't getting any younger and ...'

'You!' incredulously, 'in the role of old lady's companion!'

Georgie shrugged. Let him believe what he liked. She settled herself in the window-seat, from where she would be able to see Dr Grey's car coming up the village street.

'Anxious to get rid of me, Georgie?' Niklaas had always been disconcertingly perceptive where she was concerned, and she flushed with mingled embarrassment and anger. Anger that he could still read her so easily, anger that forced her into straight speaking.

'Yes, but you must have known I would be, even before you came looking for me. The fact that you're injured doesn't make any difference to that.' Except that it made her feel dangerously softer towards him. Compassion for the injured was something they had always shared. Unable to meet his eyes, she continued to stare out of the window, aware that he was scrutinising her profile.

'Your parents told me where to find you,' he said abruptly.

'Oh!' Georgie felt betrayed. 'I made them promise ...'

'I was able to convince them,' he said smoothly,

'that it was in your interests to break that promise, in the circumstances.'

'What circumstances?' she began, when a sharp breath, as in a violence spasm of pain, came from the direction of the couch, and she turned her head.

Niklaas's eyes were closed, as he fought his battle with agony. Unable to resist this opportunity of looking at him, really looking at him after such a long time, Georgie stared hungrily. He hadn't changed much in two years. He was a tall, powerfully built man, and the sheepskin coat, which it had seemed wiser not to remove, served to emphasise this fact. Yet Georgie knew what the coat concealed—a large man, yes, but with no spare flesh on that muscular frame. His hair was a coppery brown, a thick and vigorous growth, and she knew just how it felt to exploratory fingers. She shivered a little at the memory. His face was all strong planes and angles, his nose straight, his jaw uncompromising. Just now his mouth was drawn into the hard lines of pain, but in any case it was always a firm mouth, only the lower lip betraying a hint of sensuality. Even though, for the moment, he had been rendered helpless, Niklaas still seemed to present a threat, to fill the small room with his aura of sexual magnetism, his physical strength.

Engrossed in her nostalgic inventory, she had forgotten the closed eyes, and now she realised these were wide open again, watching her sardonically. At once she jerked her head away, staring once more through the leaded panes of the window.

'I thought you might have fainted,' she muttered, in an attempt to explain away her intent gaze.

'I notice you didn't rush to revive me.' Mockery still twisted his mouth.

'No, I didn't. If you *had* fainted, it might have been the best thing. At least you wouldn't have felt any pain for a while.'

'That worries you?' he enquired smoothly. 'That I'm in pain?'

It did, in spite of everything, but she wasn't going to admit it.

'The only thing that's bothering me is your presence. So you might as well tell me, before the ambulance comes, why you're here, because it will be your last chance. I don't want you to come near me again.'

She was glad then that he was incapacitated, as his eyes narrowed, his face contorting, not with pain this time, but with anger.

'Just think yourself lucky I can't get my hands on you right at this moment! I'm not that easily deterred. I'll be back, Georgie. This is only a reprieve. I want the answers to some questions.'

'You'll never come near me or lay a finger on me again,' she told him, defiantly. 'I'll ask for police protection!'

His voice issued this time as a husky whisper, deliberately calculated, she knew, to play upon her sensitivities.

'I can remember a time, we can both remember a time, when the touch of my hands wasn't so abhorrent to you!'

Oh God, he was so right. She *could* remember that touch, the feel of his arms about her, the sweet demanding pressure of his mouth, the hard contact of his body, and she'd thought that two years without a sight of him had enabled her to forget. There was a glint, a fever in his eyes that almost made her wish she could put the clock back, know once more the possessive slide of his hands over her, arousing and exciting her to a need that had taken so many long, weary months to stifle.

'It's been a long time.' He had always had that uncanny knack of voicing her thoughts. His eyes were half-closed. Was it with pain, or desire? But no, Niklaas hadn't desired her any more. That was a part of why she'd left Marula, but only a part.

She felt an urge she hadn't known in a long time, a ridiculous urge to cry, but she mustn't relax her guard before him. Once he had gone, she could indulge herself in that relief. The worst of it was that she knew that if he hadn't been incapacitated by his fall and had taken her in his arms, by now all her resistance would have been beaten down, her response full and ardent. Humiliatingly, she still wanted him, and in that humiliation still hated him.

It was a good thing she was already sitting down. She doubted if her legs would hold her at this moment. Steadfastly she kept her eyes on the road, willing Dr Grey's car to appear. Miraculously it did, a sturdy, old-fashioned Morris, bulldozing its way over the treacherous road surface, skewing slightly sideways as he braked outside. Relieved by the necessity for action, Georgie was capable of movement now, hurrying to open the door.

The doctor looked tired, she thought compassionately, as he nodded a greeting and preceded her into the cottage's small living-room.

'Never known such a winter in all my years of practice,' he grumbled. 'Practically every case I've been called out to in the last fortnight has been a broken limb,' and to Niklaas, ''Fraid we'll have to sacrifice these trousers, old chap.'

Georgie turned her head away, again Niklaas's pain was hers, as a deft movement of the doctor's scissors slit the well-cut slacks, exposing a swollen, twisted limb. She was used to animal ailments, to treating creatures in pain, but this was not just any anonymous patient, this was Niklaas.

'Hmm, not much doubt about that.' The doctor's assessment was swift. 'Telephone, Georgie, please. Let's see if there's an ambulance available.' Waiting, he drummed impatient fingers on the table-top and spoke to Niklaas. 'I must warn you, unless it's a very complicated break, there's absolutely no chance of keeping you at the hospital. We're overcrowded as it is. If the X-ray shows a straightforward break, we'll have to put a cast on and bring you back here.'

Georgie gave an involuntary cry of protest, and the doctor raised his eyebrows.

'I thought Mr van der Walt was a friend of yours? And you've a spare bed,' he asserted with positive knowledge. 'It'll be some while before I can discharge your aunt—long enough for this young man's bones to heal. Don't worry, there won't be any real nursing. With luck he'll be able to hobble about in a week. And it'll be company for you, Georgie. Your aunt's been concerned about you and young Susan, all alone here.'

Susan! Georgie could feel her cheeks flushing, was aware of Niklaas's interested gaze.

'Right!' Dr Grey dropped the receiver back on to its rest. 'Ambulance is on its way. Best get that bed ready, Georgie. Unless I'm very much mistaken, your friend will be back in a couple of hours at the outside.' He strode towards the door, missing Georgie's muttered, 'He's no friend of mine.' But

Niklaas heard, and she knew he wouldn't miss the chance of retaliation, so she followed the doctor to the door, making a great display of seeing him out, even accompanying him to his car.

'Do I have to have him here?' she pleaded, as the doctor lowered himself into the driving-seat. 'I don't really want to.'

His weary face was briefly upraised to hers, making her ashamed of burdening him with her problems.

''Fraid so. Before this bad spell is over, there'll be more elderly people like your aunt filling the wards. It's becoming a nightmare, hoping that a bed will be vacated before another occupant needs it.' A wry smile twisted his tired features. 'If you're worried about the proprieties, I doubt the young man will be any threat to you for a day or so. Susan any brighter?' he added to Georgie's worries by enquiring. 'That child hasn't a strong chest, you know. Pity you can't take her to a warmer climate.'

The ambulance was prompt, but Niklaas's departure on a stretcher was only a temporary reprieve for Georgie's quivering nerves. He would be back, and by then she must be ready to face him with a little more poise, be ready with glib answers to his questions.

There was no way, if Niklaas was to be brought back to the cottage, that she could hide Susan from him. He knew now of the child's existence. Could she pull the wool over his eyes, or would there be some feature of her daughter's face that would strike in him a chord of recognition?

In an almost trance-like state, she prepared tea for herself and Susan, then went next door to reclaim the toddler. The child's cough seemed harsher, she noticed anxiously, eyes too bright, her cheeks overheated, and the doctor's words returned to haunt her.

'Cheryl's daddy played bears with us,' Susan informed Georgie, then, fretfully, 'Why haven't we got a daddy?' Why indeed?

Georgie soothed the tired child. Easy to placate a toddler, but what would happen in years to come, as Susan grew up? There would be no facile escape then from the truth.

Tea, as always, was a long-drawn-out meal, with spills to be mopped up, questions to be answered, the day's events to be talked over, but it was finished at last. With luck she would have Susan bathed and in bed before her unwelcome visitor returned.

The child was sound asleep almost as soon as her burnished curls mingled with the chocolate fur of her beloved teddy bear. But for a long time Georgie stood staring down at her little daughter, a worried frown between her eyes. Susan's persistent cough troubled her, and the usually lively toddler didn't seem to be regaining her normal energy. This was the first time Susan had been ill, and Georgie fretted, knowing that if anything were to cut short this small life her own would never again be as fulfilled.

At last she tiptoed from the bedroom and down the stairs, avoiding the step that creaked. There was still no sign of Niklaas returning. Perhaps they'd kept him in after all. Perhaps his injury was more complicated than the doctor had thought. She could not be so unkind as to hope so, but the thought of being here alone with him, for several days, terrified her. Besides, what would the neighbours think? Impossible, in this tiny village, with its efficient grapevine, to keep Niklaas's presence a secret. Soon everyone would know that Georgie Jonson had a man, albeit an injured one, staying with her, and in her aunt's absence!

Georgie realised that she was pacing the room restlessly as she had been used to do, for hours on end, when she had first returned to England. Perhaps a long, hot soak in the bath would relax her. It was hours now since Niklaas had been taken away. It was very unlikely now that he would be brought back.

Feeling a little calmer after the bath, she rubbed herself dry. As she did so, the full-length bathroom mirror reflected her slender figure, the gentle contours of her hips, her flat stomach. She had kept herself in good physical shape. Outwardly there were no signs that she had borne a child. Could she pretend Susan was a niece? A friend's child? No, of course not, when Sue's speech was so uncompromisingly clear, when 'Mummy' was the most overworked word in her vocabulary. Adopted, then? Single women were permitted to adopt these days. That might work. But would Niklaas ever believe that she, a self-declared rolling stone, would voluntarily tie herself down?

Oh, damn him, damn him! Coming here, opening up old wounds, posing problems she hadn't thought to face. In her room now, the gilded hands of her bedside clock pointed to nine. No point in dressing again, she would treat herself to an early night, a read in bed. There was an extremely interesting article she hadn't had time to read, concerning research into a mysterious new disease which affected cats. She had just settled herself comfortably against the pillows and found her place in the journal, when the front doorbell rang. Damn! Oh, it couldn't be! She slid out of her warm, comfortable bed, pulling a robe tightly round her silk-clad figure. Let it be someone else, she pleaded inwardly as she ran downstairs, a neighbour needing to borrow something. Vain hope!

The ambulance men supported Niklaas in the doorway.

'Bring him in,' Georgie said unsteadily. 'It's the room at the back, on the right.' Esme's bedroom was downstairs, while Georgie and Susan occupied the two small rooms under the eaves.

She saw the ambulance men off the premises and rebolted the door. Then, reluctantly, she returned to stand in the doorway of what must now, temporarily, be considered as Niklaas's bedroom.

'Anything you want, before I——?'

'Yes!' The reply came promptly, she thought resentfully. If he imagined she was going to be constantly waiting on him—— 'Perhaps you could take away one of these pillows? Why do hospital people always insist on jacking you up like a broken-down vehicle?'

To do as he asked, it was necessary to lean over him, and her pulses jumped erratically. She felt too defenceless, clad only in a thin robe and nightdress. Her nervousness was not misplaced. As she made to remove the offending pillow. Niklaas hands darted out, gripping her shoulders. It had all been a ploy. He'd known only too well that of her own accord she wouldn't have come near him. Was he aware of his own strength, that tomorrow she would have bruises in her soft flesh?

'We'll have that little talk now, Georgie!'

'No. We've nothing to say to each other.' She tried to pull away, but he was too strong for her.

'Don't try my patience. I'm short on it just at present, with this damned leg playing me up.'

'Surely they gave you painkillers, sleeping tablets?' Temporarily diverted, she ceased her struggles and stared at him, concern creasing her normally smooth brow.

'Of course they did. But they're not one hundred per cent effective.'

'When can you take some more?'

'Is that consideration for my welfare,' he jeered, 'or the knowledge that they'll put me out for a bit?'

'Both,' she snapped. 'Since you ask.'

'The consideration I doubt. You've never had any consideration for my feelings. The desire to see me out cold is more in character. But I'm not taking any more pills, until you've told me what I want to know.'

'And if I refuse to answer? I don't have to tell you anything.'

'You'll talk,' he said grimly, and before she could guess his intention he had pulled her down on top of him, the move so accurate that her mouth was against his, his lips hard, punishing, as he released her shoulders only to wrap her in a tight, cruel embrace.

Lips compressed against the demand of his, Georgie wriggled violently, twisting futilely against the steel trap of his arms. But just being this close to him was disastrous. She could feel desire mounting in her, and she mustn't respond, she mustn't.

His mouth slid away from hers, found the hollows of her throat, the sensitive places behind her ears, his hands were sliding posessively over the soft, silken-clad shape of her. In another moment he would have unfastened the belt of her robe, giving him easier access to what he sought. And Dr Grey had said Niklaas wouldn't present any threat in his present condition!

'Your leg,' she gasped, 'you'll make it worse.'

'It couldn't feel much worse than it does, just as I couldn't feel any more strongly than I do now.' He ground the words out, but to Georgie they seemed to speak of anger rather than desire. Nevertheless, the unwanted heat continued to rise within her, an effect he had always been able to achieve. He was straining her even closer, and despite clenched teeth a moan of pure need escaped her. It had been so long. Scarcely knowing that she did so, she allowed her hands to slide up around his head, plunging her fingers into the thick vitality of the coppery hair, arching herself against him in urgent demand.

But as she succumbed his mood changed, his grasp loosened and she was able to lift her head a little, to look at him wonderingly, pleadingly. His face was a taut mask.

'Still the same old Georgie!' Slightly breathless, revealing that he himself was not unmoved, his tone was still contemptuous. 'How many men have there been in the last two years, I wonder?'

Able to release herself, she struggled upright, turned away, unwilling to let him see the tears that glinted in her eyes, threatened to brim over. At the door, all movement was arrested by his voice, a voice suddenly bleak, unutterably weary, pain-filled.

'I'll have those tablets now, if you'll be kind enough to provide a glass of water. There's a package in the pocket of the hospital dressing-gown.'

She fetched water, found the tablets and handed them to him, silent under his hooded stare. His eyes continued to condemn her over the rim of the glass, and as he set it down he electrified Georgie by saying:

'What did you do with the child, Georgie? Did you get rid of it, or did you have it? Is this Susan that child?'

'I . . . I . . .' He *knew*. How? Dirk had *promised*!

'I've come to find that child, Georgie, if it still exists, to take it back to where it rightfully belongs, Marula. And now for God's sake get out of here and go to bed,' he muttered. 'I find I can't stand the sight of you any more tonight. I wish there hadn't been any necessity for me to find you. You've always meant trouble, and by hell I've copped a packet this time, you *and* this leg. I'll see the damned child in the morning.'

He couldn't take Susan away from her, he couldn't! Like a palsied old woman, Georgie dragged herself up the stairs to her room. The bed was cold now, as cold as her heart within her, and she huddled miserably under the bedclothes, trying to get warm, unable to sleep because of the chill winter that seemed to have penetrated not only the room but her whole being, and because she could not stop herself going endlessly over Niklaas's words. Why did Niklaas want to take Susan back to Marula? Why had Dirk waited this long to tell him the truth? Why not when she had walked out on him two years ago?

CHAPTER NINE

GEORGIE slept restlessly, and she was up early.
Going into Susan's room, she found the child's bed
empty. For a moment she stood transfixed. He
couldn't have . . . not without her hearing him.
Besides, he was in no fit state to leave here on his
own, let alone with a toddler.

As she ran downstairs, the sound of Susan's
laughter reassured her. She burst into Niklaas's
room, relieved, yet chagrined to see her small
daughter perched on the end of his bed. As Georgie
entered, Susan turned towards her, her small face
alight.

'Look, Mummy, I've found a daddy. You always
said I could have one some day.'

'Did you indeed?' The laughter had died out of
Niklaas's face as he glared at Georgie. 'And whom
had you in mind for that honour, especially since
you were still married to Dirk?'

'I had to explain to her, why she hadn't . . .'

But Niklaas was looking at Susan again.

'There's certainly no doubt about whose daughter
she is.' At his words, Georgie froze. 'She has his
eyes, but fortunately she hasn't inherited that awful
marmalade hair.'

Georgie felt herself go weak with relief. Dirk
hadn't said anything. Niklaas thought Susan was
Dirk's child, just as they had planned. But the
excitement, the laughter, had brought on Susan's
hacking cough, and Niklaas frowned.

'You don't seem to be too expert a mother.

What's wrong with the child?'

'She's only had a cold,' Georgie said defensively. 'It's just taking her a while to shake off the cough.'

'I'm not surprised, in this ghastly climate, and this cottage may be picturesque, but it's not exactly draught-free. It's a good thing I found you when I did. What that child needs is some warmth and sunshine.'

'Maybe,' Georgie snapped, 'but *not* in South Africa. You can't take her back there. You've no right.'

'I've every right,' Niklaas replied calmly, 'as her guardian and the executor of Dirk's will.'

'D-Dirk's *will*?' An icy chill cascaded down her spine.

'Yes,' then mockingly, 'you should have stuck around a little longer, Georgie. Marula is yours now, until Susan comes of age.'

'You mean Dirk ...' Georgie's throat worked convulsively. 'He—he can't be ...?' She hadn't been in love with Dirk, but she'd been fond of him, grateful to him, until she'd found out how he'd deceived both her and Niklaas—and this was Georgie's first real experience of loss. No one close to her had ever died before. 'Wh-what happened? Was it an accident?'

'No. It was partly due to his old complaint.'

'I never knew what that was. He ...'

'Neither did I,' Niklaas said grimly, 'until after the post-mortem. Dirk was a coeliac ... You know what that means?'

'I—I think so. It—it's a chronic wasting disease, isn't it?'

'Yes—due to a sensitivity of the intestine to gluten. The body fails to absorb the proper nourishment from its food. That accounts for why he was so thin—and always sickly.'

'But I didn't realise it could kill you.'

'I think it's a rare occurrence,' Niklaas agreed. 'Most sufferers are put on a special diet and as long as they stick to it . . . But Dirk was an extreme case. He'd had various operations in his teens, apparently, something else I never knew—to remove certain parts of the intestine that weren't functioning or were diseased.'

'Poor Dirk.' Georgie's throat worked convulsively. 'B-but you said it was only partly due to that . . .?'

'Yes—it was pneumonia that finished him off, poor devil. He got caught, about six weeks ago, in a freak storm miles from Marula—in an open car.' The words were coming painfully, as though Niklaas genuinely mourned the other man's death. But Niklaas had hated Dirk de Vries . . . 'The car got bogged down and he was stuck for hours. When a passing motorist found him, he was already suffering from hypothermia—the pneumonia set in later. His system just didn't have the stamina to resist it.'

Georgie was crying. Whatever Dirk had done to her by his lies, and she knew he'd been prompted by his own hopeless love for her, he hadn't deserved such an awful death.

'Oh, come!' Niklaas said curtly. 'Don't pretend to be grief-stricken! If you'd been in love with him, you wouldn't have walked out the way you did. Why did you just disappear like that, Georgie?'

'Because . . .' She stopped, blew her nose fiercely. The truth was dangerous. She couldn't tell Niklaas how Dirk had deceived her, that her marriage had been one of convenience, on her side at least, or why it had been so convenient.

'Never mind,' he shrugged. 'It's not important just now. What is important is that we get back to Marula as soon as possible. The lawyers must see Susan, and Reita too is anxious to see her grandchild.'

'But . . .' Georgie frowned, perplexed. Reita knew that Susan wasn't Dirk's child.

'Until Dirk's will was read, she had no idea of Susan's existence.'

'But Dirk said he'd told his mother . . .' No, that was a dangerous statement to make too. 'I can't leave here,' Georgie said desperately. 'Aunt Esme's still in hospital, but when she comes home, she'll need me to . . .'

'All taken care of,' Niklaas interrupted. 'I've been to see your parents, made them see they must tell me your whereabouts. They'll be here tomorrow, and they're prepared to stay indefinitely for as long as your aunt needs care, or alternatively, for her to make her home with them.'

'Who the hell do you think you are?' Georgie demanded fiercely. 'Coming here, arranging other people's lives?'

'I've told you who I am,' Niklaas said quietly, 'the executor of Dirk's will, and one of Susan's legal guardians. Obviously he felt you might prove to be an irresponsible mother.'

'But that's not true!' Georgie cried. 'I've devoted every moment of my time to her. I love her.' I love her even more because she's *your* child, she added inwardly.

'Then prove your concern for her welfare by getting her out of this cold, damp cottage and back to Marula. I guarantee that cough will disappear within days.'

When they arrrived next day, Paul and Maggie Jonson reinforced Niklaas's arguments.

'You can't deny the child her inheritance,' Paul pointed out, 'whatever your personal feelings, and Niklaas is right, the climate would be better for her.'

'But I'd be so far away again,' said Georgie. She could remember only too well how it had felt to be unhappy in a far country, and nothing would have changed.

'We haven't seen that much of you these last two years,' Paul said inexorably. 'We've missed you, I won't deny that, we shall miss you. You're still our daughter, but you're a mother yourself now. You *must* put Susan first, not only her health, but her future.'

But it wasn't Susan's inheritance, Georgie thought, a week later, as she sat beside Niklaas in the aeroplane that was taking them to Johannesburg. Susan wasn't the rightful heir to Marula, and Georgie had no idea what other relatives Dirk might have. She would have to ask Reita, and ask the other woman just what she was up to, since she knew as well as Georgie that Susan wasn't Dirk's child.

Very suspicious was the uncharacteristically warm welcome she received from Reita de Vries, her doting manner towards Susan. There were fond comparisons made with Dirk's childhood, points of resemblance sought and found. But there was no opportunity for Georgie to take her mother-in-law on one side before the family lawyer was summoned to meet her and to read the will once more for her benefit.

'To my wife, Georgina,' Dirk had written, 'for

her lifetime only, I bequeath Marula, which I know she genuinely loves, to be held in trust by her for her heirs.'

Bewildered, Georgie shook her head. Dirk must have known his will wasn't legal. Marula was entailed to his direct descendants, or failing that . . . There was a final paragraph which, apparently, no one, not even the lawyer, understood, and Georgie could offer no explanation.

'I also leave her my apologies for the way in which she was misled, and beg her to believe that the fault was not mine. I leave it to her heart to determine what course she should follow.'

'Mrs de Vries,' the lawyer paused in his reading, 'have you *no* idea at all of your husband's meaning?'

'No, she hasn't,' Niklaas interrupted, 'but I have.'

Every face in the room was turned towards him.

'Then why,' the lawyer asked with some irritation, 'didn't you declare your knowledge at the first reading of this will?'

'Because,' Niklaas's tone was grim, 'I wanted Georgie to be here, I wanted her to know just who did deceive her.' Suddenly, unexpectedly, he turned on Reita de Vries. 'It was you, Reita. You were up and about that morning, the morning I left for the Cape to see Lysette. You found the message I'd left for Dirk, and for some devious reason of your own you destroyed it, gave him your own version instead. I know that much. Dirk and I had a lot of time to talk during his last illness. A lot of things, including his relationship with Lysette, a relationship which you and my dear wife falsified and exaggerated, became a lot clearer.'

'I've no idea what you're talking about,' Reita blustered, her heavy-jowled face flushing an unbecoming shade of purple.

'Oh yes, you have. You wanted Dirk to think I'd walked out on Georgie, you wanted her to think so too. You deliberately broke up my first marriage, and you wanted to make darn sure I didn't marry again.'

The lawyer gave a dry cough.

'Before we . . . ah . . . proceed to these personalities, may I just deal with the final clause of this will?' and as Niklaas made an impatient gesture of assent, he continued: 'I appoint, as chief executor of my will and as one of the child's guardians, Niklaas van der Walt, my cousin and only male relative.'

It took a few seconds for this last sentence to hit home, and when it did Georgie thought she understood everything, or almost everything. She looked up at Niklaas with horror-stricken eyes.

'I never knew you and Dirk were cousins,' she faltered, enormous eyes begging for his belief.

'Distant cousins,' he supplied. 'We didn't advertise the fact.' His tone and expression were ironic. 'Would it have made any difference if you had known? No, you couldn't have guessed Dirk had such a short time to live. If it hadn't been for the accident, he might have been alive still.'

'Oh!' Georgie knew his implication was not lost on anyone present, and she felt anger engulf her.

The lawyer coughed once more and shuffled his papers, suggesting that he would like to leave now. Reita de Vries escorted him to the door, seeming only too pleased to make her own escape, and Georgie was left alone with Niklaas.

If she hadn't married Dirk . . . no, if Dirk hadn't deliberately led everyone to believe that Susan was *his* child, Marula would have gone to Niklaas, under the terms of the entail. Georgie knew she was in an appalling dilemma. Morally, she should reveal the truth. But then everyone would know. Oh, damn everyone! What she meant was that Niklaas would have to know that Susan was his child.

Not necessarily! Dirk had told his mother that the child was Hendrik Beit's. Georgie had never understood his motives for that lie. She did now, of course. To his mother, who knew the details of his illness, he could never have claimed the child as his. But that lie could come in useful, if Reita would support her. But would she? If Reita had wanted Niklaas to inherit Marula she would have spoken up by now. All the way along the line, Reita de Vries had been working against Niklaas, so help seemed unlikely from that quarter.

Georgie shook her head in despair, and in an effort to clear her thinking processes. She mustn't rush into any decision. If she revealed the truth about Susan, first Niklaas might not believe her, and if he chose to do so she, Georgie, would never be sure if it was genuine belief, or whether he had seized upon it as a way of claiming Marula. Either way, obviously he was going to insist on Susan remaining. He might even fight Georgie for possession of the child, for she would no longer have any right to remain.

'Well, Georgie,' Niklaas was staring at her curiously, 'it's all yours now. No elation? Has Marula lost its magic for you?'

'No,' she said slowly, and it hadn't, but its magic wasn't the kind that could put things right for her, and for Niklaas. It was no use making a direct approach to the subject of *his* right to inherit. Instead she said: 'Why did you keep so quiet about being Dirk's cousin?'

He contemplated her for a long time before he answered.

'I didn't deliberately hide the fact. The subject just never arose. As I told you, the relationship was a distant one, and Dirk and I had been at loggerheads for some time.' His chiselled features softened. 'Poor Dirk,' he said quietly. 'I wish I'd known sooner just how sick he was, that I'd believed him when he denied having an affair with Lysette. But Lysette herself wanted me to believe it, and Reita wanted me to believe it.'

'Why does Reita dislike you so much? Why should she want to harm you?'

'Jealousy?' he speculated. 'Certainly she resented my closeness to Oom Klaus. Her own son had been sickly right from birth. She probably knew better than he did just what his life expectancy was. Much as she hated Marula, it did provide her with financial security, and if I were to inherit she would have lost that base to fall back on.'

How little Reita de Vries must know Niklaas, Georgie thought. She was certain that, shown the proper affection by his aunt, Niklaas would never have seen her suffer, either the loss of a home or financially. But Reita de Vries judged people by her own standards.

'Yet she moved out when Dirk and I were married.'

'She came back immediately after you left! She's probably hoping you'll be soft enough to let her stay on, until she feels like another jaunt, hoping she'll be able to dominate you the way she did Dirk.'

'You said she resented your relationship with your uncle? You got on well with him, obviously?'

'Yes.' Niklaas's face took on the closed-in expression which she recognised as his defence against expressing any kind of emotion. 'He took me in when my own parents were killed. I was only three at the time, and as I grew older he taught me everything I know about Marula. He paid my way through veterinary college and I repaid my debt to him. I intend to go on repaying it by living and working here. Can you understand that?' he said it almost challengingly.

'Of course,' said Georgie. Niklaas would never admit it, but it wasn't just a question of monetary repayment. It was a debt of love. He had loved Klaus de Vries like a father. In fact, he was probably the only father-figure Niklaas could remember.

'Reita once said, during one of their rows, that Klaus thought more of me than of his own son.'

'And did he?'

'Of course not! Klaus wasn't like that. He adored Dirk. It was a constant source of unhappiness to him that Dirk would never be fit enough to share his work here, as I could.'

So in fact, Georgie thought, whatever Reita de Vries's feelings on the subject, her husband at least would have been more than happy for Niklaas to inherit Marula, if and when the time came.

'Well, I must be off.' Niklaas's, manner was remote, matter-of-fact. Since that one moment, at her aunt's cottage, when he had taken her in his arms, he had said no word, given no sign that he was in any way still attracted to her. And yet was there any significance in his parting words? 'You know where to find me, if ever you want me.' He paused briefly on the threshold, as though expecting— hoping?— for a reply, but as yet Georgie hadn't the right words, and she could only nod, her eyes large and wistful.

She might not have the right words yet for Niklaas, but there was no doubt in her mind just what she must say to Reita de Vries. She waited until Niklaas's tall figure was out of sight, the sound of the jeep's engine telling her he had really left. Then, having placed Susan in the care of the comfortable, middle-aged wife of one of the scientists, she went in search of the other woman.

Reita was in her bedroom, the room she had always occupied when she'd been mistress of Marula. Dirk and Georgie had never used it, remaining instead in Dirk's suite of rooms.

'What do *you* want?' Reita demanded, as Georgie entered with a perfunctory knock. There was no sign of the gushing cordiality with which she'd greeted her daughter-in-law on arrival. 'Just because Marula is yours, does that mean you intend to walk in and out of my room just as you please?'

'But it isn't your room any more, is it?' Georgie began.

'Oh, so you intend to throw me out again, as you did when you married my son?'

'You left of your own accord,' Georgie reminded her, her tone deceptively mild. She wasn't ready to use her big guns yet. 'You were very anxious, for some reason, that I *should* marry Dirk, even though you didn't like me.'

Reita remained silent.

'You were afraid I might marry Niklaas instead, as I would have done, if you hadn't lied to Dirk and, indirectly, to me.'

Still the bulky woman's lips were sealed in a grim line.

'And we both know, don't we,' Georgie continued inexorably, 'that I have no right to Marula?'

Now Reita did speak, nervously, jerkily.

'You're still Dirk's wife. His death doesn't change that.'

'True,' Georgie conceded, pausing deliberately. Reita de Vries deserved to suffer the agonies of doubt a little longer. She had made other people suffer enough, including her own son, though she would probably deny that, claim that all she had done had been prompted by maternal love and not her own irrational dislike of Niklaas. 'But Dirk had no right, legally, to leave Marula to me. Marula is entailed.'

'For Dirk's child, though . . .'

'But Dirk told you, Susan wasn't his child!'

'No . . . no . . .' The fading marigold hair was displaced from its careful coiffure as Reita shook her head. 'He didn't. He . . .'

'Yes, he did. He told you the child was Hendrik's, and you seized on that, didn't you? You were ready to go along with the deception, let everyone think my child was Dirk's.'

Again Reita was silent, but her face worked violently, making her ugly.

'Dirk lied to you,' Georgie told her, and again Reita's head shook vehemently.

'No, he couldn't have done. He wouldn't have lied to me, his own mother. He wouldn't have d. . .'

'Were you going to say "he wouldn't have dared"?' Georgie asked sweetly. 'That I do believe. It's probably the only true word you've spoken. Dirk didn't dare lie to you, except in this case, when he wouldn't have dared to tell you the *truth*.'

'But it had to be Hendrik's.' Anger made Reita suddenly careless. 'My son wasn't lying to me. I *know*, because I know Dirk was incapable of father. . .' She stopped abruptly.

Georgie's heart gave an enormous leap. Reita had confirmed her suspicions, put into her hands the one indisputable item of proof she needed. The coeliac disease from which Dirk had suffered was sometimes the cause of infertility and it seemed this had been so in Dirk's case—and that was something that could be *proved*, by applying to his doctors.

'It *was* Hendrik's child,' Reita whispered. It wasn't an assertion now. She was begging Georgie to confirm it.

'Susan is Niklaas's daughter,' said Georgie.

'No!' Reita de Vries held out her hands, as if she would ward off the knowledge Georgie imparted.

'Oh yes, and now I know how to prove it to him. I'm going to tell him so. Marula should have been Niklaas's. It's *going* to be his.' She didn't wait to hear Reita's reply, if the other woman was even capable of making one. Instead, she turned on her heel and marched out of the house, heading for Dirk's Land Rover, still parked under the trees that shaded his house.

Poor Dirk. She felt her eyes sting suddenly. She hadn't cried since she'd first heard of his death, its tragic circumstances. She hadn't cried at the reading of the will—she'd been too shaken by its revelations. But now she could truly grieve for the man who had so briefly been her husband—for Dirk himself, as someone to whom she had been grateful, and though she hadn't been in love with him, she had been fond of him, until Reita's lies had rebounded on him—fond of him for his own sake as well as what he had done for her in marrying her.

Thank God that now she knew he, as well as she, had been wronged. She only wished she could have known the truth sooner, while he was alive, so that she could have thanked him for what he had done for her, for all that he was still trying to do, even after death! Transfixed by this thought, Georgie sat with her hands resting on the steering-wheel. Dirk's intentions were clear now, his final message to her explained. He'd *known* she would do the right thing, at whatever cost to herself, that she wouldn't let Niklaas be the loser, and he'd hoped this would bring Georgie and his cousin together. Would it? Even though she now had solid proof to offer Niklaas that Susan was his, it didn't mean he still loved, or wanted, *her*.

Never mind! Unknowingly, Georgie's shoulders squared, as her hands tightened on the steering-wheel. Dirk had provided this opportunity, and she wouldn't let him down. She'd take it, whatever the outcome, even if she got hurt in the process. She owed it to Niklaas to tell him the truth, all of it, just as she'd told it to Dirk. Yes, even including the fact that she loved him. And she owed it to *Dirk* too, to clear his name of his mother's lies.

She would tell Niklaas, leave him to digest the facts. After that it was up to him. She looked at her wristwatch. How swiftly this eventful day had passed! By now, unless he was overloaded with work, Niklaas should be back at the bungalow. She started the Land Rover's engine and engaged first gear.

There was no jeep parked outside, but as always the door to Niklaas's bungalow was unlocked and Georgie walked in. She was trembling almost uncontrollably at the thought of what she had to do, and it was almost a relief to find him not here yet, giving her a chance to compose herself.

Nothing had changed. Time might have stood still for two years. The dust might have been the same dust. Georgie sank down into one of the shabby chairs, then leapt up again as she heard the sound of an engine. She was standing rigidly, chin up, face determinedly set, as Niklaas walked into the living-room, but her lips were set too, to prevent their trembling, so that she found it impossible to take the initiative as she had planned.

'Georgie!' He acknowledged her presence, but her name, his inscrutable expression, gave her no help.

'I . . . I . . .' she began, but could get no further.

'Why don't you sit down?' he asked, and she could have sworn that, just for a moment, there had been an amused quiver to his lips.

'Thanks,' she said shortly, the suspicion of mockery causing a steadying spurt of anger. 'But I'd rather stand. What I've got to say won't take long, then I'll go.'

'Oh, I don't think I could allow that.' He moved a little closer. 'You have a habit of doing rash things, or disappearing, when I let you out of my sight.'

'Niklaas, please be serious. I . . .'

'I *am* serious, never more so. Sit down, Georgie!' Bemusedly, she watched his hand close round her arm, which for an instant seemed remote, disconnected, as if it belonged to someone else. Then feeling flooded back as into a numbed limb, as the warmth of his fingers penetrated and he drew her towards his own chair, a chair large enough to hold two.

'Niklaas, no . . .' she protested, as he drew her down with him and began to kiss her, very comprehensively, as if determined not to miss one inch of her face, her neck, his hands preparing a way for more intimate caresses.

'Niklaas!' His name was just a weak breath on her lips this time, as she felt herself in danger of succumbing to this insidious attack. 'We *have* to talk.'

'Later,' he murmured, 'much, much later.'

Georgie wanted nothing more than to be able to give herself up to his lovemaking. But if she did so she could never be certain of his motives. Might he not want Marula so much that he'd be prepared even to marry his cousin's widow, to gain at least temporary possession? See if he'd still want to make love to her when she'd told him the truth! Determinedly she wrenched herself free, returned to her deliberate stance in the middle of the room.

'I *must and will* say what I came here to say,' she told him defiantly, though she was shaking in every limb, as much from the effect of his kisses as from fear of his reaction.

Resignedly he sprawled in his chair.

'Yes, I can see that! I could see the determination in your stubborn little face the moment I walked in, which is why I . . .'

'Niklaas, please, do shut up and listen, while I still have the courage to tell you that I . . . that Susan . . .'

'That you love me and that Susan is my child,' he electrified her by saying. 'Right, it's said, now come back here.'

But Georgie couldn't move.

'You *knew*!'

'Only quite recently. Dirk told me. He told me an awful lot during his last illness. I know everything about you there is to know, Georgie—*everything*,' he emphasised as she looked doubtfully at him.

'Then why,' she demanded indignantly, 'have you been so horrible to me, in England and since we got back here? If you knew all the time . . .'

Niklaas's face twisted a little.

'You don't think I enjoyed it? I've never wanted to hurt you, Georgie. But would you have come back to Marula if I'd told you the whole story? Wouldn't you have suspected my motives? I had to goad that independent streak of yours because you *had* to hear the truth from the one who's been against us all along, Reita. You had to come to me willingly, with your mind clear of all doubts. And you have.' There was nothing indolent about him now. He had risen, and was coming purposefully towards her. 'I said I knew everything, but the one thing I still need to know is whether you're going to be sensible, for once?'

'Sensible?' It was hard to be rational, even, when Niklaas was holding her like this, when the pressure of his body was telling her things that *she* needed to know, that he still desired her. That much was very evident. But love?

'It wasn't very sensible of you to go to bed with a delirious man. Supposing I'd been the unscrupulous type? Or suppose I'd never remembered what took place?' His voice was light, teasing.

'*You* could never be unscrupulous,' Georgie told him softly, her hands compulsively framing his face, trying to restore order to the unruly auburn hair.

'It wasn't very sensible of you,' Niklaas's breathing had accelerated, his words coming jerkily, 'to think that I wouldn't want my own child, wouldn't want you, not very sensible to rush into a panicky marriage with Dirk.'

'It seemed to be the only sensible thing to do,' Georgie argued bemusedly. It was becoming harder to think logically, her pulses beating to the race of his heart.

'And then you did another silly thing.' As if

absentmindedly, Niklaas was caressing her hips, pulling them harder against his own. 'You ran away, and nobody, including me, could think why.'

'Was Dirk very hurt?' Georgie faltered, and as Niklaas nodded her eyes filled with tears. 'I wish he hadn't been. I wish I'd known how good he really was.'

'He understood finally.' Niklaas's words, his arms, were comforting. 'When we got together, pooled our information, found out how much it conflicted *and* found out the author of our confusion . . .'

'I've only ever hated one person in my life as much as I hate Reita de Vries,' Georgie said savagely. She didn't have to explain, Niklaas knew whom she meant. 'When I told my stepfather I was coming out here to work, he reminded me that cats have claws. He was warning me to be careful of poor Dirk. We know who the dangerous one really was.'

'Reita can't do us any more harm,' Niklaas told her. 'So,' his hands stroked her breasts, 'are you going to do the sensible thing?'

'Which is?' whispered Georgie, though she was blissfully sure now that she knew the answer.

'Marry me, of course,' he confirmed, 'because I love you.'

'Oh yes, Niklaas, oh yes, please. What are you doing?' as he lifted her in his arms and began to carry her towards the door.

'This time,' he said smugly, 'I am *not* delirious, and I plan to savour, to remember everything about you, for myself, my dearest love.'

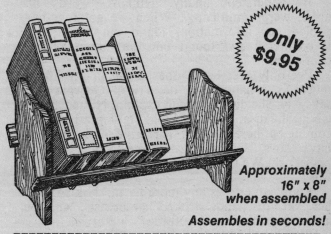

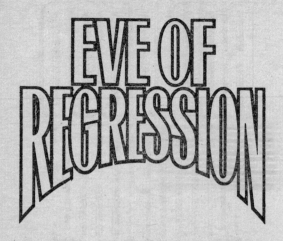

**A soaring novel of passion and destiny
as magnificent as the mighty redwoods.**

He could offer her the priceless gift of security but could not erase the
sweet agony of desire that ruled her days and tormented her nights.